Cat's CRADLE

Dale Mayer

CAT'S CRADLE: BROKEN PROTOCOLS 3
Beverly Dale Mayer
Valley Publishing Ltd.

Copyright © 2014

ISBN-13: 978-1-773363-86-8
Print Edition

About This Book

Lani and Liev Blackburn have slid from the frying pan directly into the fires of Hell. When they uncover insinuations of a dangerous conspiracy that can be traced directly back to the foundations of society and permeates every part of life as the world knows it, they realize that to expose this evil is to shake the Earth to its core.

One by one, people begin disappearing. If not for Liev's twisted, genius brother Milo and Lani's talking cat Charming Marvin, the two of them would also be missing—or dead. But someone is still playing games, stalking Lani and everyone connected to her, and the cat's cradle web they're weaving is becoming impossible to escape. Unless they can find a way to expose this massive cover-up and who's behind it all, they'll become the next vanished.

Books in This Series:

Cat's Meow
Cat's Pajamas
Cat's Cradle
Cat's Claus
Broken Protocols 1-4

Sign up to be notified of all Dale's releases here!
https://geni.us/DaleNews

Protocol 3:2:2. You will in no way misuse your authority or position or the trust placed in you—particularly if those actions are to selfishly enhance your own authority, position, status, and/or wealth.

Chapter 1

LANI SUMMERLAND BLACKBURN walked restlessly through the living room and kitchen. Her new life two centuries in the future had taken a strange and ugly turn. The problems besetting her since her arrival should have been over—instead things were likely to go from bad to horrible. Figures. Murphy's Law had somehow followed her to this time period. Like, how did that work?

She was desperate to calm the tension vibrating through her. The police had come and gone. As for the lawyer who'd tried to kidnap her, his remains had been removed. Life supposedly could now return to normal. Whatever that meant. She had no normal left. This time jump had come with no warning or preparation for what could happen next.

Life had hit her sideways, and she was still sliding. She'd done the best she could, and Liev had been a godsend. Then again, he'd been the reason she'd been plucked out of her nice happy little life into his—as a gift for him—compliments of his uber-brainy kid brother.

Since she'd first arrived, they had had nonstop

trouble. From horrible pain to debilitating exhaustion to heated passion between her and Liev. That last part had been a bonus. But between that and the people coming after her, life had been a dangerous roller coaster.

And she needed off.

As they still hadn't gotten to the bottom of this nightmarish kidnapping scenario, they weren't safe yet. And, if anyone found out that the time-travel trick had resulted in her overgrown Persian cat now talking like a fluffy Einstein—and getting worse every day—would more people be after her and Charming Marvin? More than likely they'd both be locked up in a lab for the rest of their lives. That was so not going to happen.

Was it any wonder she needed a break from this stress?

Determinedly, she turned to face Liev. He sat, his chin propped up on his fingertips. Eyes closed, deep in thought. And she could just imagine what was going on in his incredible brain, one that matched his incredible body. Sex aside, Liev had turned out to be a hell of a good man. She walked closer.

"Are you okay?" She sat down beside him, happy when he opened his eyes and smiled. Something was still so weird knowing that this man was her husband. They'd only known each other a few short days. He'd married her to keep her safe; yet now she couldn't imagine life without him. Her cheeks heated as she remembered some of their best times together.

His gaze warmed. He cocked an eyebrow and murmured, "What are you thinking about?"

She gave a slow, intimate smile. "Good times." She paused, then added, "And I was wondering about …" She let the words trail off, not sure how to phrase it.

"What?" He reached out and slowly ran his fingertips up and down her arm. "If you need something, you only have to ask for it."

"I need to get away. From here. From all this nastiness."

He frowned and damned if a bit of fear, insecurity maybe, sat in the back of those deep purple eyes.

"Not from you," She reached out to stroke his cheek.

The shadow in his eyes lightened, and he sat back to study her.

"I was just thinking that I have a lot to learn. We need time together, yet people are after us."

He nodded. "All true."

"I was wondering if we could go away for a week or two. Where it might be safe for you to take me out and to show me life here. Where making a major gaffe won't attract much attention. Where we could spend a little time together. Where every move won't be watched. Where I can learn ports, and shopping, and …"

He held up a hand. "I get the idea."

"It's a great idea," Milo piped up. "We could all use the break."

Liev faced her, a question in his eyes. She gave a small laugh and nodded. Of course Milo could come. And no way would she go without Charming, her walking, talking miracle feline.

"A good idea as long as we all go," Charming said, as if reading her mind. "It's too dangerous for us to split up. Besides"—he hopped up on the back of the chair and butted his head against her shoulder—"who'd look after me?" His huge golden eyes stared at her in worry.

"Not going to happen." She stroked his silky back, leaning over to kiss the top of his head. "I wouldn't go anywhere without you."

"Or Milo," Liev said with a laugh. "It's a good idea. We both have a few things to take care of first, not to mention deciding on where to go. In theory, we could leave tomorrow."

She brightened. "Thank you. That would be perfect." She grinned, thinking about how easy that had been and added, "Besides, today is almost over."

Charming snorted. "What time are you on? It's barely after lunch." And he gasped, his eyes rounded into huge glowing marbles. "*Lunch.*"

"No," Lani said. "You had lunch."

"But I had an early lunch, and that means it's snack time." He turned his flat face toward Liev and deepened his tone. "You did order treats for me too, right?"

"Wow." Lani rolled her eyes. "It's hard enough for poor Liev to adjust to a talking cat without that same cat trying to order him around. Remember your manners."

"Ha. He's doing fine." Charming shot a leg into the air and proceeded to clean the back of it. "Soon he might even start obeying those orders."

She smiled and reached out a hand to stroke her four-year-old pet.

"Liev, as much as it's a good idea, I think we need to solve this problem first," Milo said. "The leads are hot right now. If we leave, these assholes will go under, and we might never catch them."

"I was actually thinking about sending you three away, and I'll stay here and deal with this," Liev answered.

"Oh no." Lani shook her head, adding in a flat tone, "All of us or none of us."

He frowned. "Milo has a good point. This has to stop." He reached over to cover her hand. "If we leave, they'll just be waiting for us when we return."

"So we solve this first and then leave. Personally, I'm thinking a beach." Charming dropped and sprawled along the back of the couch. "I'd like some more sand."

Lani snorted. "Maybe you could just get a litter box instead." She exchanged a laughing look with Liev, remembering the last time Charming had come close to sand. "If that's the case," she said, returning to the problem, "what must we do to resolve this mess permanently? I hate the idea of always looking over my shoulder."

"It seems to have started with Johan. We need to

find Johan and whoever was behind my lawyers' attempts to kidnap you. Hahn said that Gina had gotten him into this trouble, and *they* probably tortured Johan's name and location out of her. So we also have to find her killer. I'm hoping the two are the same man or group of men."

Johan was Liev's friend who lived in the top apartment—or used to. Lani had never met him. He was on the run from the authorities now. "Okay," she said. "That makes sense, but how we do that?"

"That's my part," Milo said around the straw in his mouth, as he sucked up something bright green. "Finding them, in theory, is no problem, but stopping them is."

"Because we don't want to involve the authorities?" Lani asked.

"Partly, but they are involved already," Liev said. "Two dead lawyers cannot be glossed over." He reached out and tugged her into his lap. "We need you safe."

"I need all of us safe," she muttered, "but how?"

LIEV CUDDLED LANI close. He'd do anything to keep her from harm. Had already done several things he never believed he would have done. But they'd been necessary. "We're good at what we do. We'll find the responsible parties." He squeezed her gently. "I promise."

When she looked up at him with those huge eyes filled with uncertainty, he repeated, "I promise."

Milo came up behind him. "Sounds like it's time to get back to work." He brought up the big countertop 3-D monitor.

"I need treats first." Charming groaned. "I can't help you until I regain my strength."

Lani laughed. "Ha." She nudged Charming's large sprawling belly. "You're getting fat."

"I am not fat. Well, maybe a little, but I'm cuter this way." He stretched out a right paw and offered the underside of his belly for a scratch. When she obliged, he moaned.

Liev shook his head. "He's something else. I'll put on coffee and help Milo."

At the sound of coffee, Lani swung around so he could get up. He laughed. "You are as bad as your cat. Your treat is just in liquid form."

She stretched out on the space he'd vacated and smiled. "In that case, we both deserve treats."

"Finally." Charming moaned, as if in major pain. "Treats. I need treats."

Milo snorted. "How about a booster? Whoa! What do we have here?"

Liev raced over.

Lani twisted to lean over the back of the chair. "What did you find?"

"I'm not sure." Then Milo pinched his lips, and his hands moved faster and faster.

Liev stepped back and watched his brother work. It was rare to see him in the zone to this extent. His brother was sheer magic. And, when he was on the hunt, he was lethal. His hands flashed. The screens shifted too fast for his eye to see what they were. The monitor buzzed with the speed of the activity. It blurred in front of him. Then Milo made a slashing motion with his hand, and everything froze.

Lani made a strangled sound from behind them.

Liev could only imagine what she thought. Nothing even close to this in terms of home computing had existed in her time. Bigger, faster, and more complex computers were at his office, but not by much. By the very nature of Milo's genius, his baby brother needed tools available at all times. And typically the best that could be had. That meant building their own super-computers. Not a problem, but many of their inventions went way past computing. That's when they got into trouble with the Council and the cops.

Milo leaned closer.

Liev stepped in to look. "What is it?"

"An intersection of paths."

"Whose paths?"

Milo tapped the top of the screen, drawing Liev's eye to the faces. Both Defino brothers' images sat on one side. On the other side sat the two dead lawyers, Gina and Hahn.

"So you've tracked all their paths?" Liev asked Milo.

"To this one spot." Milo tapped the monitor frozen

in place. "At the old shipping docks."

Liev frowned. "That's the turf I'd expect from the Defino brothers, but not the lawyers."

"Except," Lani interrupted, "Hahn said something about not liking where he was being forced to take me to." Lani walked closer to study the screen. "So maybe that's the headquarters. The boss man would be in a location like that, wouldn't he?"

"Only part-time," Liev said. "They'd have a home base somewhere a long way removed from that hellhole. Likely at the topmost end of the scale."

Her face fell. Then lit up again. "That would make sense. Could that be Johan? He lived pretty well in this building. You have no idea what he did for a living, but it sounds like it was just on the edge of legal."

Liev shrugged. "If we could track his path to the same area, then I'd say definitely. But as he's gone underground …"

"What about his known friends and associates?"

"He doesn't have any." Milo looked at his brother. "Does he?"

Liev looked from one to the other. "I don't know. I don't know him that well."

"Then maybe that's where we should start looking. Everyone in his circle. See where those paths intersect?"

Milo raised his eyebrows at Lani's suggestion. After a quick glance at Liev, he swept his hand back the other way, unfreezing the monitor. Immediately the screen loads flashed and sparkled as they moved at light speed.

Lani faced Liev. "I guess that means he's on the hunt again?"

Liev smiled. "Seems like it."

"So does that mean coffee and treats are back on the menu?"

With a smile at their tenacity, Liev walked over to the wall, where he started coffee. "I guess it does."

While he waited for it to finish, the house alarm went off. Lani gasped, her hand going to her chest. He reached out to her. "It's all right. We have company. That's all."

She took a deep and shaky breath. "Okay. I'll go back in the pod room then."

"You don't have to." He was already walking toward the door. "Not if you don't want to."

"Actually, I wouldn't mind." She gave him a wan smile, reminding him how tired she was. What she'd been through already today. "A short nap, with Charming, would be nice. I'm feeling *peaky*."

"Okay then." He watched her carry on down the hallway; Charming, somehow knowing what she was up to, followed close behind. Lani looked tired, melancholy. Taking her away from all of this was a great idea. She'd only been here a few days, but they'd been brutal. The alarm went off again.

"Liev? Are you answering that?" Milo asked.

Giving his head a shake, he said, "I've got it."

At the door, he looked outside. Damn, another Council henchman. At least the suit and close-cropped hair denoted henchman. He could only see the back of the guy's head, since he appeared to be looking behind him, as if waiting for someone to join him. Not unexpected considering the break-in and death this morning. But Liev had hoped it would be over, at least for today. Like Lani, he was tired and fed up. The alarm sounded again.

Gritting his teeth at the visitor's arrogance to keep hitting the alarm, Liev went about accessing the security system. The alarm went off one more time. "I'm coming. You don't have to keep pressing the damn button."

Finally he unlocked it and pulled the door open. And stared in shock at the man standing in front of him.

Johan.

Chapter 2

LANI OPENED THE healing pod. Charming hopped up and froze. His whiskers quivered. She sat down on the side and yawned. She had to admit, she really could use a nap. The morning had worn her out. She slumped backward, spread her arms, and closed her eyes. She giggled when she felt the pod automatically shift and move under her as it adjusted to her sideways position. "Nice, huh?"

Charming didn't answer. She ignored him. She was so tired. The pod was always so welcoming. Nothing like warmth on your back to soothe and ease the tension inside. She was one step away from falling asleep now.

"Lani?" Charming asked.

"*Hmmm?*" She rolled over and tucked her knees up higher. "What?" She yawned and felt herself drifting deeper and deeper.

"Did you hear who just arrived?"

"No." And she didn't care. Her body relaxed a little more. Boy, she needed this. Just as she drifted off, she heard Charming's response.

"Johan."

The word percolated through her brain, then slammed into her consciousness. She bolted upright, barely missing the pod lid as it lifted automatically ahead of her movement. She hadn't had a chance to think with so much going on, but, upon reflection, it seemed like the pod was doing more things. As in learning her, adapting to her and her likes and needs.

Nice.

And creepy.

"Did you say that was Johan at the door?"

"Yes." Charming stared at her, his eyes impossibly round. "Why would he come here?"

"No good reason that I can think of." She sat on the edge and worried about the problem. "Can we hear the conversation?"

"Audio on," Charming said.

Immediately Liev's voice slipped through the ceiling. "Johan? I don't understand. Why are you here?"

Milo didn't give Johan a chance. "Whatever his reason, it's a bad idea."

"Milo, give him a chance to explain."

Silence.

A strange lilting voice rasped, "Thanks for the opportunity, Liev. And, Milo, for all your brains, you need to learn a little more about human psychology."

Charming snorted. "Why? He's got brains, and that means he doesn't need anything else."

"That's not true," she whispered. "And we should probably be quiet in case they can hear us."

He shot her a look of disgust. "Whatever." He lay down, rolled over, and curled into a tight ball.

"Great. You wake me up, and now you get to sleep." She glared at the sleeping cat. "How is that working for you?"

"Quite well. If you'd be quiet, I could actually get some rest."

She threw herself down and curled around the bright orange body, hugging him close. "Do you think I should go out there?"

"No. Absolutely not." The alarm in his voice reassured her.

"Right. That's not a good idea, is it? Then Johan will know for sure that something is odd about me."

Charming shuddered. From his twisted-up position, he opened his eyelids and glared at her. "DO NOT GO OUT THERE." He lifted his head, as if to make sure she was listening. "Liev will handle it. Johan knows we are here. Let them deal with it."

"But"—she stared down into the flat face—"what if the brothers are in trouble and need our help?"

"Not going to happen." He closed his eyes and went back to sleep.

"It might." She lay her head next to his. "You never know."

"I know." He snored gently.

"But what if you're wrong?"

No answer. She closed her eyes and relaxed. Before she realized it, sleep swept her away.

LIEV STARED AT his old friend and wondered what the hell had happened. The fun-loving guy was gone. This man had a hard edge to him, a well-used look to his face, and his eyes? It seemed they'd seen too much. A second closer look showed heavy bruising on one side of his neck. He held himself slightly hunched over, one arm protecting his potentially damaged ribs.

This was not good.

"What happened to you, Johan?" Liev waved him inside, watching his friend move gingerly.

He winced. "I look that bad, huh? I could use my damn healing pod right about now."

"Sit down. I'll get you a drink." Ignoring Milo's disgust and instinctive wariness, Liev poured a stiff drink into a glass and brought it over to Johan. "Here."

Johan took it gratefully and tossed it back. He shuddered and then said, "Thanks, I needed that."

"I can see that, but why?"

His friend slouched back, stiffened, then straightened slowly.

"You're hurt," Liev said quietly. "Is it bad?"

"No. Just took a beating. On an ordinary day, no problem, … but I blew up my pod." He gave Liev a lopsided grin. "Don't suppose you'd like to return the favor and let me borrow yours?"

"No," Milo snapped. "For all we know, you're behind the problems we've been having."

Johan's eyebrows shot up. "What kinds of problems?" He looked at Liev. "I told you to marry her to protect her."

"I did."

"Well, congrats, man." Johan slapped Liev on the shoulder, then groaned at the resulting pain it caused. "That's great. You're a married man now." He shook his head, like he couldn't believe it. "She must mean a lot to you."

"She does."

"When do I get to meet her?"

"Never," snapped Milo. "Someone is after her. We're making sure she's safe."

"Why the hell would anyone want to kidnap her?"

Milo narrowed his gaze. "I didn't say *kidnap*."

Silence.

Johan put up both hands. "Hey, I'm not sure what's going on here, but I have nothing to do with whatever is happening. I've been on the run and got into a little trouble myself."

"Why?" Liev asked curiously. "What happened to you?"

"I thought I took everything I needed with me. Instead"—he grimaced—"I left something behind. I'm here to retrieve it."

"Have you been up there yet?"

"No. I was hoping to use your tube to get there, take a quick look around, grab what I needed, and then scoot back down here undetected." At Liev's surprised look, Johan added, "I could go through the little rooftop garden you use."

Liev shook his head. "And here I thought that area was private. Secret."

"Nothing is secret anymore." As he spoke, he stared straight at Milo. "Haven't you learned that yet?"

Milo stared back at him silently, not showing any give in his expression. After what they'd been through, and the secret experiment Milo had accomplished in bringing Lani here, keeping his work private—top secret—was paramount. Milo would do anything to protect his inventions. And, if Liev didn't quite trust Johan, no way Milo would.

He was suspicious of everyone.

Yet, Liev had to concede, Milo appeared to have taken to Lani and to Charming just fine. More than just fine. Maybe he'd run compatibility tests across everyone's profiles. Yet another thing to ask his brother.

Later.

Liev refocused on the issue at hand. "You can use the tube to get to the rooftop."

Milo started to protest, took one look at Liev's glare, and shut up. He stormed from the room.

"He's not a happy chap," Johan noted.

"We've had a rough morning." Talk about an understatement. Liev half expected to see more Council henchmen here soon enough. Not to mention cops. They would have more questions. No way they wouldn't. Hell, Liev had a lot more questions himself.

He studied Johan carefully. "So you had nothing to do with the bug that came in with my healing pod?"

"What?"

His shock was real at least.

"Don't you have an automatic bug sweeper here?" Johan's lips twitched.

"Yes, we do. But the bug was built to detach at some specific time or at a prearranged signal, then move to a different location in the room."

That shut Johan up. He sat back slowly and stared. After a long moment, he shook his head. "What the hell. Whose bug is that?"

"Milo is tracking it down. At the moment, we have no idea but suspect it belonged to the Defino brothers."

"That's not good." Johan stared into space, but didn't sound surprised at the brothers' name. Then they had a long rap sheet. "I had my pod customized, you know? So it would only transmit specific innocuous data to the database."

"Really?" Too bad Johan hadn't mentioned that fact earlier. It would have saved Liev a lot of worry. "That's a great idea."

"Not good enough. Something still went wrong. It did make me a popular fellow for a long time though." He grinned, a rueful smile of remembered parties and women, ... so many women. "I had the same person rig it that you bought yours from."

"How do you know who I got it from?"

A harsh laugh slid out of Johan's throat. "Only one

supplier has the audacity to do something like this."

"Do you have a name?"

"Nope. No one does."

"Damn." Liev walked over to the window. He wasn't getting much help here. If he knew Milo, his kid brother would already be out searching the airwaves for information on Johan. Nothing like siccing someone who didn't trust another to dig out dirt on them. "Paul Defino broke into my house today."

"What? I didn't hear anything about that." Johan stared.

"Oh, you will soon. My lawyer was killed during the mess."

"Wow." Johan let a long slow whistle slide through the room. "Okay, now *that* I definitely don't know anything about."

CHAPTER 3

LANI DRIFTED IN and out of the pod's warm healing rays. Some of the conversation from the other room filtered in. Not enough to truly understand what was going on but enough to stop her from going into a deep sleep. *Figures.* She yawned and rolled over to face Charming in another attempt to drift off.

He stared at her. And damn, those whiskers were quivering. His large globe eyes stared into hers, and his small ears peeled back along his head, as if to hear better.

"What's the matter?"

"Johan says it's not him."

"What's not him?" She blinked, trying to process the short, terse message. "None of the mess is?"

Charming gave a small headshake, sending his fur billowing out.

She frowned. "Then who is behind all this?"

"No idea. And we need to find out."

"Agreed." She lay here, thinking, when Johan's voice filtered in again.

"Are you sure I can't use the healing pod? Just for a few moments. I'd sure like to feel better. Honestly, besides the jaw, I'm pretty sure a couple ribs are broken." His painful gasp could be heard.

It didn't sound like he was faking it. And that made her feel guilty as hell.

"Sorry, Lani is sleeping in it."

"Sleeping? Dude, she should be warming up your bed, not snoozing in a healing pod." Amused envy laced Johan's voice. That sounded more like the party-giving Johan that Lani expected to hear. The sexy party animal looking to score and not understanding his buddy's reticence.

There was a heavy silence. Lani winced. If the guy was hurt, it was the right thing to do to give it to him. Did she get up and walk out, as if she had just woken up? How else would they know she was awake and willing to leave the safety of the pod? "Charming, can you contact Milo?"

One eyelid slid open. How did Charming manage to look insulted? "Of course."

She didn't want to be seen. She didn't want to meet any more strangers. Any more bad guys. "Can you tell him that I'm leaving here and going to Liev's room, so the pod is free for Johan?"

"Yes." Charming stood and arched his back. "If that's what you want."

"Are you coming with me?" She sat up gently and slid to the side of the pod. "Or are you going to stay and visit with Johan?"

He gave an odd mewl that she took for a snort, then

he jumped down. To the speaker system, he said, "Message for Milo only." She stared as he said, "Lani and I are switching to Liev's room. The pod is free for Johan." He twisted, gave her a look, and, when she didn't understand, he sighed. "Open door. Stealth to remain on."

The door opened silently.

Damn. She hadn't even realized the door was voice-controlled. Hating the things she didn't understand, she motioned for him to go first. "Lead the way so we can't be seen."

He shrugged. "Configure to keep us in stealth." And he walked out.

She followed, a low burning irritation with a touch of envy washing through her. "How am I ever supposed to get used to you knowing how to do all this when, only a couple days ago, you didn't even talk?" she muttered.

"We've been over this. I could always talk. You're the one who just learned how to understand." He groaned. "Now if only you'd learn the rest of this stuff faster."

He ran down the hallway, and she had to pick up the pace to keep up with him. With his tail in the air, he looked like a normal feline. Under that pouf of orange fur, he was anything but.

Still, that mess could be laid at Milo's feet.

Charming disappeared up ahead. She entered a room and came to a dead stop. The door closed silently behind her. She gasped. She was inside a huge chateau-type room that could have come from anywhere in the Swiss Alps. The open beam structure with log walls and wood details were awesome, but the huge bed on a platform beside a roaring fire really got to her. "Is that fire real?"

"As real as anything here can be." Charming padded over and tilted his face up to catch the warm rays.

She had to see for herself. It was, indeed, warm and cozy. She felt safe here. Comfy. She smiled. This was gorgeous and said a lot about Liev. She turned to warm her back and studied the huge bed. The coverings appeared fluffy and light. Maybe down-filled. But she suspected it was as much of an illusion as anything else here.

An illusion she wanted to believe in. The idea of sharing that huge bed with Liev? Luscious!

"Pull your tongue back into your mouth." Charming stalked to the huge bed and hopped up. He sank into the middle and turned around several times before lying down. He yawned. "This will do nicely."

"Ha. Who said that's for you?"

"Losers weepers," he replied, using an old phrase from back in her time.

She stared at him. "How is it you can adapt so quickly? Why are you not bothered about how different things are here in this time?"

He lifted his head. "What's different? Bad guys. Good guys. Kidnappings. Murders. They are the same in both times. The technology is more advanced—and so it should be. But honestly it doesn't look like humanity improved much. Besides, I only need food, love, warmth, and a cozy bed to keep my world balanced." He closed his eyes, then opened one. "It's the same for you."

Was it, she wondered. "I need to be safe."

"And you will be. Soon."

MILO CLICKED AWAY on the comp in his hand, essentially ignoring Johan and the rest of the conversation. Liev studied his brother for a brief second. Then returned his gaze to Johan. Who looked to be fading. "Do you want to retrieve your property and come back? The pod will be waiting for you."

He didn't know why he made the offer, but it seemed the right thing to do. He sensed an odd stillness come over Milo, before his clicking started in earnest. He was up to something.

Then again, so was Liev.

Johan struggled to stand, his face wreathed in smiles. "Thank you. I surely appreciate that. I'll be back in a few minutes." He staggered down the corridor to the front entrance.

Liev walked behind him. At the door, he asked, "Do you want company?"

Johan paused to look at him, considered the suggestion, then shook his head. "I'll be fine, and it will be better if you aren't seen with me. It will just get you into more trouble. Stay here and stay safe. I'll be back before you know it." And he entered the tube and disappeared. Liev stepped back inside and reset the security.

"How long do we have?" Milo asked from behind him.

"Maybe ten minutes." Liev turned to face him.

Milo had secretly followed his brother and Johan down to the hallway. "Then we'd better get moving."

"Moving where? What are you up to?"

"Setting up video in the pod room," Milo said.

Liev stared at his brother as he raced into the room where Lani lay sleeping. "Why? Wait. Don't scare her."

"She's in your bedroom. Charming told me that they'd moved so Johan could use the pod. Lani felt guilty."

Raising both hands in the air in surrender, Liev ran to catch up. Since when had Lani moved? "How did they even know about Johan being hurt?"

"Charming turned on the audio in the pod room. They heard the whole conversation."

"Sweet." He entered the room to find Milo tinkering with the comp on the wall. "How long do you need?"

"More than ten minutes," he muttered, tapping the console quickly. "I'd really like to know why he wants to use the pod. Oh, he's hurt all right. But, while he's in here, is he going to retrieve information on us? Will he send messages from our location? Is he really badly hurt? Or did he pay someone to rough him up to add some weight to his story and to get him into the pod?"

"He looks hurt. I'm sure the pod would help heal him." Any number of pods were available to Johan, but not as many were unregistered. If he used a registered pod, then his name would be sent to the databanks. He could expect a convoy of ComBots and police to be at his side within minutes. Here, he could stay undetected.

"Do you believe his story?" Milo asked.

"No. I don't." Liev added, "But it is quite possible that he is looking to retrieve something he missed from his place."

Milo shrugged. "I don't trust him."

Liev said, "Neither do I."

CHAPTER 4

L ANI CURLED UP in Liev's bed. It felt wonderful. And yet so right. Special. Illicit. Which, considering she was married to the man, was just plain stupid. She sank a little deeper into the covers, enjoying the feel of Charming kneading her belly. They'd had lots of mornings in the past where it was just the two of them. Time together to enjoy a late morning spent in bed. Time to spoil each other and to gain the comfort each offered so freely. Times had changed. In more ways than one. "It's been tough, hasn't it, Charming?"

The kneading paused. "In some ways."

She smiled. "It's nice that we can really talk now."

"Yep."

"Do you think …" She had to stop. What she was going to say sounded stupid.

"What?"

"Nah, it doesn't matter."

"Except, if it's bugging you, it does matter."

She gave a small laugh, startled at the wisdom coming from his mouth. "I shouldn't let it bother me."

"And again, that has nothing to do with it. Just because we shouldn't think about something doesn't mean we don't. And, if it's in your mind, then far better to share it."

True. She said in a thoughtful voice, "I just wondered if any of the enhancements Milo added to our transport came to me. Or if you got all of it."

"Them."

"*Them?*" She twisted slightly to look at him. "You mean, you received more than one enhancement?"

"I don't know that. I do know he added more than one. It's Milo. How could he resist?"

"Yeah." She sank back into the pillows thinking about it. "He'd think it would all work out perfectly as he had planned anyway."

"Of course, and, for the most part, it did."

"Does it bother you that you are communicating at the level you are now?"

"Yes. It's just much harder to get my beauty sleep," he grumbled from somewhere in the center of the curled-up ball of fur he'd become. "Everyone wants to talk."

She smirked. "Sorry. I'll be quiet again."

"Yeah, but not for long."

Reaching out a hand, she gently stroked along the curve of his back. "Maybe not, but I do love you, and I'm so glad we're together."

His purr hit diesel-engine level in seconds.

Content, she lay here and dozed, wondering what other enhancements Milo had added to the two of them—or just Charming. And had they worked?

Supposedly there was a high incidence of failures with enhancements. Apparently Mother Nature still ruled.

The door opened. Liev walked in and looked around. "Hey, how are you feeling?" he asked, after spying her in his bed.

She realized he had to be worried, considering she could barely be seen under the mound of covers. "I'm fine. Just tired." On cue, she yawned. "Is Johan in the pod?"

"No, he's gone to his place to retrieve something. He'll be back in a few minutes."

"Okay, at least it's ready for him."

"Thanks for that. We did use his pod when we needed it, so …"

"Understood. It's the right thing to do." She shuffled back up against the headboard, so it was easier to see Liev. She was surprised to see him standing in the middle of the room. "Uhm, I hope it was okay to move in here? I know I didn't ask, but I wasn't sure what else to do."

"Of course it is," he rushed to reassure her, yet stood stock-still.

She stared at him, loving the warmth that filled his huge eyes. "Good. Then why are you standing in the middle of the room like that?"

The heat in his eyes flared. "Because I don't dare get any closer." His legs brought him a step closer regardless. He clenched his fists.

She raised an eyebrow. Her toes curled.

He dropped his gaze slowly down her face and neck to rest on her breasts, plumped up from the bedding she'd tucked around herself to keep warm. "Because joining you in here is exactly where I want to be, but Johan will be back in a few minutes. And Milo is working on something that might need my help."

That made sense, and it reassured her. "You should hurry back."

He swallowed hard. "Working on it."

But he stayed frozen in place. Then, with a low groan, he said, "I'm leaving. I'll be back soon."

She raised her other eyebrow. He raised both hands in frustration, turned on his heel, and raced out. She grinned. "Nice to know he's just as affected as I am."

"You're both idiots," Charming murmured. "Now do you think I could get some sleep?"

LIEV TORE OUT of that room before he jumped into that bed and made love to Lani. He'd dreamed of her in his bed, lying beside him. Lying under him. On top of him. Any position would work as long as it involved Lani.

"Whoa, Liev. What's going on?" Milo stood in the hallway studying him. "Is everything all right?"

He winced. Definitely time to control his unruly thoughts and wayward body. "I'm fine. Just realized you might need some help." Yeah, as lame excuses went, that one topped the cake.

And, if the look on Milo's face was anything to go by, he agreed. "*Right.*" He walked toward the kitchen. "Maybe coffee? Or a cold shower?" he murmured as he slipped past his brother.

"Ha. Coffee will be fine."

"I'm not so sure. You don't need more stimulants," Milo said, a grin on his face.

Liev glared at his brother. "No, I don't. But the coffee would be good regardless. I'm sure Lani would love some after all the attempts to get her a cup just to keep getting interrupted. And maybe we have time for a cup before Johan gets back."

He walked over and pushed the button, choosing an espresso blend. He might not need the stimulant, but he could use the shock to his system. Lani was a powerful drug all on her own.

"Speaking of which, I expected him back already."

Liev turned around to face Milo. He frowned as he looked down at his own comp. "How long has it been?"

"Fifteen going on sixteen minutes."

Liev made the mental calculations in his head. "He could have trouble finding what he needs to find. If it's even still there. He's hardly late yet." He walked over the counter and the big 3-D screen. "Did you track his movements?"

"No tracks to show how he got here. Unfortunately. Then again, he's spent a lifetime living this way. As for where he went, he did take the tube to the top floor.

From there? I don't know."

"Can you hack into the system? See if any working computer eyes are in his place that we can access?" Liev thought about what Johan had said before. "Johan said he had eyes on most of the building. Said he recognized the guy who came to give Lani her tags. Knew the guy who sells the unregistered healing pods."

"Did he now? *That* you did not mention before." Milo got busy. "Would have been good if you had."

"It never occurred to me. We do the same with Johan. Well, *before* we may have."

"Yes, but he didn't come in today through the normal channels. He's keeping track of us all but not letting anyone see his tracks. And that's not allowed."

Liev grinned. Milo had a huge competitive streak. He also lived on the airways and knew how to traverse the electronic world better than anyone Liev knew of. Milo's ability to dig himself in until he found what he was looking for spoke to his stubborn nature. He had a lot of bulldog in him.

A good trait when it came to hunting. Liev left Milo to it and took a moment to check the huge backlog of emails and business issues waiting on Liev. He'd been slacking these last several days, and some things he couldn't ignore any longer. He buckled down to deal with the easiest and fastest of them. It took twenty minutes to take the cream off the top, delegate a huge portion of the other issues to his staff, and skim over the rest. Feeling better now that he knew what was backed up, he turned to the coffee he'd forgotten about. Pouring two cups, he carried one into the bedroom for Lani.

And found her sound asleep.

He stared down at the sleeping beauty curled so innocently in his bed. All he wanted to do was slide under there and curl around her.

She rolled over and opened her eyes.

He smiled gently. "Hey, did you enjoy your nap?"

She smiled sleepily. "Did you come to join me?"

"I wish." He lifted the cup in his hand slightly higher so she could see it. "I did bring you coffee."

Her eyes lit up. "That's a wonderful second-place prize." She shifted back and up, and he realized she was fully dressed, not exactly the image his mind had been busy creating. And reminded him of another oversight. "I need to get you new clothes."

She winced. "I'd appreciate it. I've been washing my underwear in the sink and leaving it to dry overnight. But one outfit does not last forever."

"Do you like the style? I can give you others, but that style looks lovely on you. And it's easy to grab you a half dozen of the same."

Her gaze widened. "Yes, please."

"Your wish is my command." He turned and walked toward the side wall of his bedroom, where he brought up the clothing program. He quickly repeated his clothing instructions but switched up the colors. As an afterthought, he multiplied the outfit by seven. That should work for the moment.

As he stacked up the goods on the bed, he got a transmission over the home security system. The robotic voice said, "A request for help has been received."

Liev straightened. "What? Who?"

"Johan Strand."

"Damn. Is he hurt?"

"I have no further information from the sender."

"But he's alive?"

"At the time of transmission."

"Well, that's something." He hated that the first thing through his mind was that Johan was dying. There'd been too much death lately. He raced out of the bedroom and into the kitchen. "Milo? I have to go check on Johan. He's sent out an alert for help."

"I'm coming with you."

"No, you need to stay here with Lani."

"Lani will be locked in here. You need backup."

That his kid brother saw himself as Liev's backup was touching and funny as hell, but Milo had proven that he could be helpful in many situations. Given the choices, Milo was correct. As long as Lani stayed inside, she'd be safe. Liev could set the security system to alert him if anyone approached. And that was a hell of an idea. "Thanks, Milo."

He ran to the front door, set up the alarm, and stepped out, Milo at his back. The two stepped into the tube and took off for Johan's apartment.

The tube disappeared as they arrived at their destination. Johan's door was locked down tight. Liev motioned at Milo to follow him to the small rooftop garden. They couldn't hear any sounds from the place. That in itself was unusual after hearing Johan's endless parties. Liev stepped over the small divider and carefully worked his way around to Johan's big rooftop patio. The place was dark and silent. The big double doors stood wide open, also unusual, but good for Liev and his brother. He wanted to race inside and call out for Johan, but Liev's instincts stilled his tongue. He felt an eerie sense that they weren't alone.

He knew the layout pretty well. He slipped inside and slid along the wall to the left. Johan's bedroom should be down the same side of the apartment. Liev couldn't hear anything, but neither could he see anything. The darkness was absolute.

Milo motioned toward a large black bar set near the middle of the room. Nodding, Liev crouched down and made his way to it.

Then they heard someone rustling around in the room next to them.

But was it friend or foe?

Chapter 5

LANI SAT UP, threw off the covers, and slid her legs over the edge of the bed. Beside her was a large stack of clothing. Different colors and designs, all appearing to be pieces of the same outfit he'd given her last time. Liev had dumped them beside her before racing from the room. He had called back as he left, "These are more of the same. Later we can sit down and pick you out different clothes."

Now she wondered at his words. Sit down and pick out some clothes? Did they have stores anymore? Or only online stores? Did he design something himself? Or did he use a design program? Input her coloring and measurements, and, voila, a whole new set of clothes? Hit the Print button, and there they were?

She paused at the idea. That almost sounded possible.

Spreading out the clothing, she smiled at the bright colors. They were the same design as the one she currently wore but with a fresh look. She loved them. A deep bronze top and milk chocolate pants were her first choice. The array of matching sexy underwear made her cry out in delight. She dressed quickly. She folded the dirty clothes and laid them off to the side, then re-stacked the remaining outfits. She looked around and realized that, of course, she saw no visible dressers or drawers. Everything would be sunk into the walls. Or compressed in such a way as to open upon command. *Multitasking space*, he'd called it. Cool idea.

And it made for a nice clean line in the room. There was little clutter, just open warm space.

Leaving the clothes stacked on the bed and feeling like every other woman with new clothes, she walked out with a skip to her step.

And found the men missing.

She wandered through the kitchen and large sitting room, with no sign of Liev or Milo. She frowned. If they were with Johan, she preferred to stay out of sight. After a moment of indecision, she refilled her coffee cup, delighted that she'd learned that much here and returned to find Charming. In the center of the bed, Charming opened one eye and stretched out a paw. In a lithe move, he rolled over onto his back.

"Charming, I can't find Milo and Liev. Can you tell me where they are? Without alerting anyone else in the place?"

He rolled over again slowly and sat up. "Audio on."
Silence.

She kicked herself for not having tried the same thing. None of this was instinctive yet. "If they're in the pod room, with stealth on, will you be able to hear them?"

"I don't know." He tilted his head and said, "Audio on in pod room."

More silence.

"Locate Milo and Liev."

A weird robotic voice said, "Liev and Milo are not on the premises."

Lani gasped. "How? When? Where are they?"

Silence.

"Oh, come on. You must track them," Lani snapped.

"Stealth is on."

"On their personal comps too?" She doubted that.

"No."

"Then send a message and ask them where they are." She added as an afterthought, "Please."

Charming made an odd sound.

She turned to look at him. "What?"

"Oh, nothing. Just good to see you learning how this system works."

"I wish," she said. "Then I'd be able to contact Liev directly."

Like magic, Liev's voice whispered from somewhere in the ceiling, "Lani, we're in Johan's place. He sent out a call for help."

"I was just worried. I couldn't find you," she admitted.

"We'll be home short—"

And his voice disappeared.

Lani stood beside the bed and called up at the ceiling. "Liev? Liev!"

No answer.

"Contact Milo," Charming instructed the house computer.

"Communication has been disrupted."

"Ya think?" Lani turned around in a slow circle, staring up the open-beam construction as if it would magically answer. "What can we do?"

The house system said, "We must wait for communication to be re-established."

"Can you tell me if their vitals are okay?"

"Their vitals are fine."

Walking toward the kitchen, she breathed a sigh of relief and raised a trembling hand to her temple. "Good, then they aren't in any danger."

"I did not say that."

"No. You didn't." She frowned, her heart sinking. "Are they in danger?"

"I don't know that."

"Of course you don't. Then who does?"

"This might help."

Lani turned around, surprised to see Charming on the kitchen counter. "What are you doing up there? No cats on the kitchen counters. Remember?"

His *get real* look left her gasping. "I'm trying to open the 3-D computer. We can track them visually in Johan's apartment this way. See if they're in trouble. Also see if they're alone."

She watched him study the granite-looking countertop. "The problem there is, we need a scan of Johan's place with that heat-seeker scan thing on." She looked surprised at the words that came out of her mouth.

Then again, so did Charming. With an odd look her way, he turned and clicked one slightly larger white spot, and damned if the 3-D computer didn't form above the counter, with Charming in the middle of it. His fur filled with the accompanying static charge, and he immediately looked like an orange cotton ball—megasize.

She laughed. "Get out of the monitor, idiot," she said affectionately.

"Hey, how was I to know it would appear instantly? There should be a three-second time delay for me to shift position."

"Well, be sure and tell Milo that. He can program that in for you."

"Ha, I'll do it myself."

"Ah, Charming, that might not be a good idea."

"Too late," he groused. "Besides, we live here now. Everything needs to be adjusted for us too."

"Right." Fascinated, she watched as he closed the system, then tapped the same white dot and moved off to the side.

He beamed at her, his marble eyes glinting through the fluff. "See? Not so hard after all."

"Wow. I look forward to seeing Milo's reaction to you tinkering with his computer."

"He'll be fine with it."

She doubted it, but that was Charming's headache, not hers. Besides, Milo gave the brains to Charming. If she had received them, she'd have respect and common sense to go with it, … she hoped.

Charming studied the multilayered holographic images in front of him. "Do you know how to find the building?" she asked.

"It *is* the building."

"Oh." She knew that. *So not.* Now that he'd pointed it out to her, she could see the different floors. Shifting her gaze to the top floor, she saw myriad yellow, orange, and red glowing places. "What are those?"

"I think those are the brothers."

"Maybe two of them are, but then who are the other two?"

LIEV CHECKED HIS comp. The house comp was listening in, but he'd gone into Silent mode. Undetectable even by the house comp. That meant Lani couldn't contact him, but any calls from her right now could get them killed. He lifted a finger to Milo and pointed to the right. Milo turned his head and frowned.

Crap, Milo didn't understand. Liev looked around Johan's lavish apartment. They'd found Johan on his bed, hurt and apparently worse than he'd been earlier. As they'd walked across the apartment to him, they'd heard someone approach from the other side.

They'd been in hiding ever since.

"Damn it, Johan, I asked you where it is. If you don't tell me, I'll have to hurt you for real."

A weird mechanical voice with a feminine tone. Liev shook his head. How was that possible?

Johan groaned in response.

"If you hadn't set your pod to self-destruct, you could be in there healing by now."

"So you can torture me more?"

"Sure. That works."

Liev couldn't see the speaker, and the voice, although familiar, sounded odd.

Milo whispered in his ear, "Voice mask."

Liev considered that. Did that mean they were dealing with a man after all? That was the more likely answer.

"What do you want to do?" Milo asked.

Damned if he knew. He had to help Johan. He could identify his attacker, and maybe they'd finally get to the bottom of this mess. That thought alone propelled him down to the room beside Johan's bedroom. He glanced inside. It was a spare bedroom. Totally bland. Odd that Johan had left it that way. In today's world, he could have turned it into so much more with just a flip of a button, so why hadn't he?

Milo joined him, glanced inside, and winced. "Boring."

"And that's what's wrong here. Johan's lifestyle was

anything *but* boring."

"So why this?"

Liev nodded.

Milo lifted the bug detector that he'd grabbed on the way out of their place and turned it on. He ran a sweep, but nothing stood out.

Liev stared at the space and wondered. Then realized it was a holograph, like he'd done for Lani's private island. Johan had deliberately made it to look like a dull, boring bedroom. So what was underneath? He slipped inside, motioning for Milo to join him. He closed the door slightly so that the flash of the house comp wouldn't alert anyone, then with half an eye on the hallway, he quickly stopped the cloaking program.

Milo gasped.

Liev turned to see an incredibly high-tech computer layout. He spun around and turned the cloaking program back on. This was what the intruder was after. And, if he was willing to kill Johan for it, Liev wanted to make sure he didn't get his hands on it.

A scream split the air. *Johan.* Liev, knowing it was the wrong thing to do, but couldn't help himself, raced to his friend's aid. He tripped around a corner and dashed into the bedroom where Johan had collapsed. Liev heard the sound of running feet as the intruder bolted outside. Liev ran to Johan's side, but Johan waved a hand at him. "Get him."

And he collapsed again.

Liev followed the sounds of running feet. Time was of the essence. If the person managed to get to the port before Liev … "Milo," he screamed, "shut down the port."

For a small apartment, it seemed to take forever to make it to the front door.

Just as the port vanished.

"Shit." He circled the port area, hoping that the attacker might have left a clue.

"Sorry, bro. There's some kind of fail-safe set. I didn't have enough time." Milo's aggrieved tone brought Liev back to his senses.

"Not your fault." He walked back to Johan. His friend looked bad. Like seriously bad. "Call for a Medivac. He needs more help than a pod."

"He's past it, bro. Look at him. He's not breathing."

"Damn it." Liev checked Johan's vitals. "Come on, Johan. Stay alive. Please." He lifted one of Johan's eyelids, but there was no response. No pulse. No breathing.

Milo stepped up and pressed his comp to Johan's tags. No responding beep, only a hum that sounded fainter and fainter, … before completely dying away. "Sorry, Liev. He's gone."

As the words left his mouth, the apartment doors slid closed, and a steel cover came down, sealing them both inside.

"What's happening?" Liev asked.

"The system just registered Johan's death. It's gone into a complete lockdown."

CHAPTER 6

WATCHING THE ORANGE dots on the big monitor was like watching a horror movie, knowing that something bad was about to happen but being unable to stop it. Lani watched the heat blobs move, crouch, and run. One appeared to be lying down, and another one stormed around. "Can we identify who these people are?"

"Not everyone." Charming pointed a claw at the two crouching. "I'm thinking those are the brothers. The one lying down will be Johan and the other one? ... Yeah, that'll be whoever Johan was calling for help about."

"You think he's a bad guy."

Charming shot her a curious look. "Is there anything in this picture that makes you think this is a good scenario?"

She studied it. "No. It looks creepy as hell."

"That's because ..." He paused midsentence and leaned closer, his whiskers quivering. "Oh, what's going on?"

She leaned forward. "That doesn't look good." The two men who crept farther away had gone down one side of the apartment, away from the other two, and had stopped inside a room of some kind. She could see a change in the energy field, but then it switched again. "What was that all about?"

"I don't know, but Johan is in bad shape and deteriorating rapidly."

She switched her attention to the prone figure and realized the heat signature, the bright orange and red colors of the others, were muted in his case. Almost faded. Something happened suddenly, and all three mobile orange dots ran in a straight line. She gasped as the first man was almost caught, but dove into … something … and disappeared off her screen. "Where did he go?"

"I'm trying to track him, but I'm afraid that might be hard to do."

"And look at Johan. His color, it's almost gone."

"The color itself will last a little while. It will take hours for his body temperature to drop so low that no color will show up."

"I'm presuming that the other two left are Milo and Liev?" At least she hoped so. She watched them go to Johan. Suddenly, as if someone flicked a switch, the entire floor of the building disappeared. It was still there, but now it only showed as a solid black bar. As if the entire floor had disappeared.

"What did you do?" she cried out. "Bring it back."

"I didn't do anything." Charming tapped the console several times, only nothing changed. That floor existed but only as a black bar. Charming sat back, stumped. "Something must be going on up there where the apartment is no longer visible."

"That's not good. Johan is in really bad shape. He needs help."

"He's past needing anyone's help. He's dead."

She gasped. "Are you sure?" she cried out. "Maybe he can still be saved. They have wonderful medical advancements here. Maybe it isn't too late."

"Oh, he's dead all right. That's also likely what triggered this blackout. Consider the secretive type of business that Johan was in. If anything happened to him, especially on his premises, some kind of fail-safe must be in effect to protect the contents. Or … to catch the killer."

"But the brothers are stuck inside." With a dead body, and, boy, did that part creep her out. "Can they get out?"

"Nah, I doubt it. It's probably locked down until someone, a prearranged someone, comes to remove information from the premises. Likely what Johan had come back to do himself."

She stared at him. "Like more bad guys coming to make sure sensitive information isn't recovered by the wrong people?"

"Something like that." Charming wandered over the counter and sniffed toward the wall. "Is there food in here?"

"Somewhere." She barely listened. Who could think

of food at a time like this? "We have to help them. They're innocent, but whoever comes to deal with this situation will suspect that Liev killed Johan."

Charming looked at her. "True, Milo doesn't look like he could kill a bug. Now Liev, that's a different story. That man looks like he could kill."

She shook her head. "What are you talking about? Liev isn't dangerous."

"Nah, of course he isn't." He snorted. "Unless his family or business are being threatened." He motioned with a pudgy paw at the monitor. "If I hadn't seen for myself that Johan was already in trouble and that a fourth person was there, I'd be wondering if Liev hadn't taken care of Johan himself."

"No way he'd do something like that," she cried out. "Where are you getting that from?"

"Uh, maybe from that can-do-what-needs-to-be-done attitude he gives off without even trying." Charming sat his paunchy bottom down and glared at the monitor. "I like him just fine, and the fact that he likes you is helpful, but it doesn't change the fact that, when threatened, Liev will do what needs to be done."

"That's a good thing," she said gently. "That's something to admire."

"So is killing when killing needs to be done." And he slid down to lie on one side where he proceeded to clean his paw.

She stared at him, his words rippling through her mind. There were times when killing was a good thing, and, if Liev was capable of protecting her from the kidnappers, well, it was a really good thing for her. Although she hoped it wouldn't come to that. Even if Charming didn't think so. "He's a good man."

"Yep, he appears to be."

"It's not as if you wouldn't kill for food."

He pinned his beady eyes on her. "I have killed for food. Why do you think I catch mice? To keep them as pets?"

She grinned. "You could go back to that. It would be good for you. A form of exercise and, just think, you wouldn't need to wait on other people to feed you. You could feed yourself."

He made a strangled sound that came from deep within his throat. "If there were mice in this day and age, I'd consider it. However, what I won't consider is exchanging my killer skills for the food that they serve me on a regular basis. Where's the sense in that? I'd do both. Not the one that takes effort at the expense of the one that is easy." With a shake of his head, he went back to cleaning.

She returned to staring at the blacked-out apartment on the top of the monitor. "We have to help them."

"I agree. Do you have any idea how?"

She winced. "We could go up there and try to open the door."

He hooted. "Really? That's the best you've got? Knowing a little about this system, chances are good you won't even find the place. It'll be on stealth mode under heavy lockdown."

"We have to do something. They'd help us." She thought about it. "Maybe we could call whatever lawyers are left at Hahn's company."

"They won't come here after two of the lawyers were killed, one on our doorstep."

"Then we have to help Liev and Milo ourselves."

LIEV HAD ALREADY done a second search for a way out that they might have missed. No such luck. From the furious pounding Milo was doing on his comp and the wall computers, he wasn't having any better luck. "This is not good," Liev said under his breath. "Johan's computer system is our best bet. Plus, I want to see what he was hiding."

"I'm working on it," Milo said. "He's got to have an override for this system."

"Yes, but it's likely to be controlled by someone elsewhere. When Johan's tag said he was deceased, this lockdown was instantaneous."

"Something important must be here. Otherwise there'd be no need for all this security."

"Information and possibly items." Leaving the main room again, Liev tossed back, "Let's keep an open mind." And he returned to the spare bedroom, Milo right behind him.

"Right." Milo reached a hand past him and clicked off the mask hiding the room's interior. Instantly the high-tech computer room showed up. Milo whistled. "Like there is some seriously good stuff here."

"Sure, but what was he into? Was it legal? Was he working for himself or for someone else? And, if it's someone else, then we need to know who."

"The system might not load with this lockdown happening." Milo had the system booting up, when he said, "Or it might send a signal to someone that we are here."

"I don't want to hear that. We need in. And fast."

"I'm working on it. You take point."

Liev stepped closer to the secondary system, surprised to find it similar to what he had in his place. Johan had to be into something secretive. Had that been what had gotten him killed?

"*Hmm.*"

"What did you find?"

"This system is connected to another system. It's trying to boot me out."

Liev waited. His brother wouldn't take that kindly. He'd be working his ass off to beat this asshole at his own game. It would also increase the danger of staying here. The need for the other party to secure this place and to retrieve or destroy what they needed was now paramount. And … he glanced over at Milo. "Careful in case of a self-destruct order."

"Oh, there will be one, but there's a reason it hasn't

gone off yet. The assholes monitoring this place need something from here first."

"Right." That made sense. That kept them alive for a little longer. It also guaranteed that a retrieval team was on its way.

And they were stuck inside.

CHAPTER 7

LANI STRODE DETERMINEDLY to the front door. They could do this. So what if she didn't know how to use the elevator-tube thingy? There had to be stairs. Even in her century, every place had two exits. Stairs made sense. Charming sat at the door, waiting for her.

"Good." She scooped him up and held him firmly. "Let's go."

"Door open," Charming said. Only the door didn't open.

Lani reached out and put her hand on the door. Nothing. "Open door."

Still nothing. "It's not coded to our voices."

"Damn. Now what?"

"We stay here?" he said hopefully.

"Nope." She turned to stare at the wall and the huge computer screen in front of her. "It means you need to add our voices or use an override system."

"Oh, great." He puffed up his chest. "As if that is a two-second job."

She smiled. "It would be for Milo."

He spun to glare at her. "That's not fair. I don't

know the system, and he does."

With a laugh, she said, "True enough. So how about five minutes?"

But he was already busy on the comp. He spun around triumphantly. "Done."

She hugged him tightly as the door opened. She stepped through, hoping she'd done the right thing. The tube surrounded her instantly. Like, how did that work? "Johan's place."

And they took off. "Shit," she said against Charming's furry head. "I will never get used to this."

He snuggled closer. "It's cool. But a little freaky."

"A lot freaky." And, as suddenly as the tube started, it stopped … and disappeared. Looking around carefully, she realized they were alone. Good. She led the way, with a couple wrong turns, to the rooftop garden. From there, she could see the whole city ahead of her. She was getting slightly more used to the scene now. It didn't scare her as badly. But it would be much more comfortable if Liev were with her. Just the thought of being left without Liev terrified her. *So not going there.*

She turned in the direction of Johan's and tried to figure out how to make her way onto his patio. Charming jumped free from her arms and raced ahead. What was easy for a cat, however, … was not as easy for her. But she made it over the cement-looking barrier and dropped safely on the other side. With only one scraped knee, she walked across the patio to the large doors. She didn't know how to get in. Steel-looking shutters hid the glass. She saw no handles. No levers. No locks. No windows. The place appeared to have locked down, like a bunker underground. She couldn't do this. "Charming, we're in trouble."

"Ya think?" He trotted alongside the house as far as they could go, until there was no side to be on. The wall dropped away to the vast city below. "That's definitely not the way." He turned, retraced his steps, and went around the other side. Following behind, she realized that led nowhere either. "So where are the fire escape doors?"

At Charming's odd look, she explained, "The second exit in case of fire so that the inhabitants can get out safely."

"Never heard of it."

"Well, I have."

"Not in the building codes of this time."

"Well, I doubt that they've managed to do away with fire, so there must be a way in or out—especially in these fancy places."

"They'd port in and out. It's fast and efficient."

She stared at him. "You know what? That's a damn good idea. I'd have a port in my house too. Actually I'm pretty sure Liev mentioned that. So why can't they port out?"

"It won't be coded for them."

"Ah, that tagging thing again."

She backed up several steps to get a better look at the building. Tall peaks and round domes, it looked like part of a duct system from her time. Then maybe a lot of those were ducts for the rest of the building. She bit her lip. Could they get in that way? Or better yet, could Liev and Milo get out that way?

"I don't like the look on your face."

She shrugged. "I was just wondering if we could get in there via the ducts or pipes." She waved at the odd structures. "Whatever they are."

"Not a good idea. We could end up anywhere."

"True." She turned to look back at the spot where the entrance should have been. "What about us porting in?"

"Not coded for us," he repeated patiently.

"Then how about the vents again …" She studied him. "Maybe you could get in."

He looked at her askance. "What? Why am I the guinea pig?"

"Because you're small, you can get into places I can't."

"I told you to lay off the bread and cheese," he murmured with a sideways look.

"Did not." She glared at him.

"Did too." He moved over slightly, as if out of kicking range.

"Yeah, you'd better move," she said in a temper. She considered his innuendo. "Am I getting fat?"

"Oh, brother." He plunked down his butt with an exaggerated sigh. "In truth, you could use some flesh on your bones."

"Not going to happen." What a stupid conversation. And, with a cat, no less. "And it doesn't change the fact that you can get into places that I can't."

"Agreed, but that also means that Liev and Milo can't follow me back out, as they are as big as you."

"Bigger."

And, boy, did he give her a look. She loved him dearly, but since he'd learned to talk, … she turned her back on him. "True that they can't follow you back out, but you could bring them something that will allow them to break out again."

"It's not a prison, and I can't carry a crowbar. Remember? I'm a cat."

"Glad you remember that." Still, he was right about being limited in what he could carry. "It would have to be something small to fit on your back."

"Like, treating me as a pack animal, … a, a, a *donkey?*"

His horrified tone made her laugh. "Exactly. Like an ass." Still giggling, she wondered out loud, "What could they possibly use in there that they wouldn't have taken in the first place?"

"Milo's new personal stealth port."

"What's that?"

"A port he can take anywhere, coded for him. So he can move in and out anywhere he wants to."

"Why wouldn't he take it with him yet?"

"No need for it. They accessed the place like normal. They probably figured they'd exit the same way.

Plus the personal port is not in the testing stage yet."

"It might be a great time to hit that stage. As in here and now to get Liev and Milo free." She couldn't think of anything better. "But, yeah. I can see how that would be a hot product for the masses."

"Some are on the market but not as transportable as this one." Charming scratched behind his ear. "Milo's portable model is ready, but he's working to interact stealth technology with it. Another military application that will make them a ton of money."

She could just imagine. It sounded ideal for military use, but she'd hate for just anyone to get their hands on something like that. No one would ever be safe. "Do you know where it is?"

"Sure. In the kitchen. He's got it on his bug computer doohickey."

It took her a moment to translate what that meant, but she remembered Milo's unusual little computer. "Wouldn't he have that on him already?'

"You'd think so, but he left it on the kitchen counter. They must have been in a hurry when they left." Charming walked to a spot in the sun and sprawled down sideways. "Not doing anyone any good anyway. I can't carry it in."

"But, if you could, do you think you could take it to them?"

At that, he slumped to the side and laid out flat. "Of course. But I'm not going back down to Liev's apartment to get it."

She glared at him. "Well, I'm not risking being separated from you as well. The chances of losing you are too great." She bent, scooped him up into her arms, and stormed back the way they came. Thankfully the door to the apartment was still open. Maybe that wasn't a good thing considering other strangers. She walked straight to the kitchen and turned in a slow circle, looking for the item. "Charming, where is it?"

He reached up, batted her cheek to get her attention, and then pointed to the counter, back against the wall. The *doohickey* blended in perfectly. She picked it up and studied it. "It's so small. And it weighs nothing. You could easily carry it, if we can figure out a way to affix it to your back."

"True. That won't be easy."

"We need something to tie around you to hold it firmly in place. It doesn't need to stay in place for long, but we can't lose it either." She faced Charming. "Is this like a prototype, the only one that Milo has?"

Charming nodded, a grimace in place. "You better not lose it. Milo will never forgive you."

"Hey," Lani replied. "I've—more or less—forgiven him for time-traveling me two hundred years into the future." She shifted her stance. "So he should remember that we did this to save him and Liev."

"*You.* Not *we.*"

"Charming Marvin Summerland Blackburn! *We* are a family. *We* work together. *We*, as in the four of us."

"Like *The Three Musketeers*, plus one?"

"That's better. Now help me think."

Charming sighed loudly.

Lani knew her baby was all heart, just under that crusty outer shell he sometimes projected to protect that soft heart of his. Luckily Liev had figured that out too. Of course Milo could care less about all the outer stuff but was totally impressed by Charming's brainpower. So it worked out all around.

"A harness would be better than something that ties," Charming stated.

"Ha. Glad to have you on board with my plan. The carrier will have to be something of a compromise, as I don't know how to make anything here and don't have any tools, like a needle and thread so ..." Her mind raced. "Elastic would work."

"Like they have that here."

Lani glanced at her own clothing. "True." And then she remembered. "But I have my old clothing." She raced into Liev's bedroom, but her twenty-first-century clothes were no longer here. Right, the pod room. She jogged over there. They had wasted enough time.

There, in a corner, she found her pile of clothes that she'd been wearing when she had arrived in this era. And in that pile ... was her bra. Her new clothes had one built in. She studied her old bra, wondering if she could make it work without cutting it up, somehow salvaging it—remembering how much Liev had liked it—but there wasn't another way, as far as she could see. She ran back to the kitchen where Charming and the small gadget sat. She opened the bread cupboard and pulled out a knife and went to work.

Ten minutes later, she raced back to Johan's place, carrying Charming and the portable port.

"I look ridiculous," Charming snapped, twisting inside his quickly tied harness—one bra cup around his belly with the new device nestled inside.

"You look great." She lowered him on the patio. "In fact, it's very stylish."

"Ha, you're just saying that so I'll do this."

"No, you need to do this to help Milo and Liev."

"I know that." He took several awkward steps, his tail flicking in sharp movements. "But you could have made it so I didn't look fat."

LIEV HAD ALREADY searched Johan's premises twice, looking for a way out. A different control server, something that would allow them to escape. Time was running out. They would have visitors soon. And, if anyone found him and his brother here, they'd soon find Lani and Charming. Not good.

He paced behind Milo and bit back the words threatening to tumble free at any moment. Milo had already snapped at him several times.

Liev had searched through Johan's communication center and had been shocked. Something that was hard to do.

He and Milo liked to keep things secret. But this? … This was scary stuff. Johan had dirt. Like major dirt on a lot of people. Liev had been horrified when he'd found the file that had his name on it, with damn-near everything detailed, including every girl he'd partied with on the list. Milo's information had been more detailed in that it had a specific set of inventions he'd created and was in the process of creating. That's what scared Liev. How had Johan known? Bugs at his place? At his office? Kept a team watching their every move. Milo will be pissed. Liev pointed out the file to Milo, who went very, very quiet. Next thing Liev knew, the information was streaming at an incredible speed. "I presume you're copying all this."

Milo nodded and held up a small storage device he always carried. "It's downloading on this and will corrupt the original when done. We don't have time to sort through it all right now."

"Have you found a way through to shut down the other system?"

"The system is not on here."

Liev sat back and thought about that. "I wonder if Johan knew."

"I don't think he did. Johan's system could have gone into lockdown any time they wanted it."

"So why didn't they do that before he booked it? Even right after he left." And then Liev understood. "They missed that window. There'd been no warning. But they set a trap in case Johan returned. So, as Johan was looking for whatever it was, he tripped a warning alarm, notifying the other computer, the one watching Johan's computer. And had a henchman here in seconds."

"Maybe, or maybe his death tripped it, like we suspected all along. Any physical or virtual tripwire or whatever could also have been set off by Johan's attacker. Once he knew Johan was dying or that we were here, he—or his partners—could have set it off remotely. For all we know, that was only stage one. Several other levels of defense are likely to come."

"Or it could be that's all there is. We'd be left here to die of starvation."

"Not likely. It would take too long."

They stared at each other.

"We need to get out of here." As the words left Liev's mouth, they heard an unidentified sound.

"Shit," Milo said, his fingers moving faster. "I need just a little more time. And why the hell didn't I bring my comp?"

Liev snuck over to the doorway and worked on the panel. He set up the same decorating disguise that Johan had originally. Instantly the same boring spare bedroom shone and damn. ... Liev stared in shock. ... He saw no sign of Milo. He quickly reverted the program, and Milo appeared again.

Deep in concentration, Milo wasn't affected by the change. Liev switched it on once more, and Milo disappeared again.

Cool. And technology he needed himself.

Now if only he could manage to do the same right now.

A long scraping sound came from somewhere overhead. "What the …?" he whispered. "It must be a rodent."

Milo's voice came through in an eerie whisper. "We don't have rodents."

"Then what is it?" Liev studied the ceiling.

A crack appeared—and not one as part of the bedroom camouflage but there nonetheless. And seconds later, Charming poked his head through.

"About time I found you."

Chapter 8

LANI WAITED IMPATIENTLY outside Johan's place, hating the fear rippling down her body. She hated being alone. She never used to have a problem with it, but now that she was in a strange world where so many things could go wrong, she had additional fears. And some of the worst ones were running through her mind right now. *Please let Charming be safe. Please let him find the brothers.*

She blew a strand of hair out of her face, and, with her hands on her hips, she slowly counted to twenty. When she hit twenty, she continued to sixty.

"Okay, he should have reached them by now." And if he had? Then what? According to Charming, Milo would be able to port them into their own home from Johan's apartment. What about Charming? Would he come back out here to find her in the rooftop garden area, or would he go home with the brothers? And what was she supposed to do? Return to Liev's apartment or wait here? Damn it. Why hadn't she gone over these details with Charming?

She shifted her weight from one side to the other and looked around nervously. What if someone else came while she was here waiting? And damn if she didn't hear a sound behind her. She dashed around the side of the building and hid.

The air tensed as odd noises crackled.

Hearing sounds but not being able to see was bad. Her mind conjured up horrible scenarios of all bad things gone wrong. Her breath caught in her chest. She flattened herself against the wall, eyes closed, … and something brushed against her legs. She screamed and danced in place.

"Ouch. Knock it off, will you? Someone will hear."

Charming! She snatched him up and clutched him in her arms. "Charming," she cried out. "You scared me to death."

"Ha, you scared me with your screams," he complained and head-butted her.

"I'm so glad to see you." She buried her face in his fur, trying to get her pounding heart to calm down; then she remembered why he'd gone in. She lifted him higher so she could see his face. "Did you make it in?"

"What about me? Are you glad to see me too?" Liev's warm, caring voice reached her.

She lifted her head, saw Liev standing in front of her, and dashed into his arms. They closed securely around her. She shuddered, then realized that Charming was squirming in the middle of the hug. She let him down before standing up to wrap both arms around Liev. Slightly behind him, she could see Milo grinning like a crazy man.

Hell, they were all crazy.

"I was so scared," she whispered.

"I wasn't feeling all that good myself." He dropped kisses down her temple and along her cheek. "Thank you for sending Charming in with Milo's personal port—a brilliant idea, by the way." He squeezed her slightly. "As you can see, it worked."

Tears burning her eyes, she tilted her head back. "I'm so glad." She glanced around the rooftop, where they were all so visible, and said, "Can we go home now?"

"Yes, absolutely."

Keeping an arm securely around her shoulders, he led her around to the tiny rooftop garden and to the main elevator.

Once inside, she breathed a sigh of relief. She held up one shaking hand and laughed. "I hadn't realized how scared I really was."

"To be expected." He squeezed her shoulder gently. "I can't believe that you did that."

"Ha. Thank Charming for that."

"You both did that. It was brilliant to choose Milo's personal port, but then you figured out that the building's ventilation system would get you around the physical lockdown. And when you put it all together, using Charming as your delivery vehicle, that was sheer genius."

Milo bobbed his head. And this time it wasn't because he was listening to his headset.

She smiled and straightened slightly under Liev's—and Milo's—admiration. Out of the corner of her eye, she could see Charming puffing up too, his head held high, as they returned home. "I am just so glad it worked. I don't know what I would have done if it hadn't."

"We'd have gotten out somehow," he reassured her.

She wasn't so sure, but, hey, she was willing to believe anything at this point. Everything was good. Well, almost good. "What about Johan? He didn't make it."

Liev flinched. "I don't know what to do about that. It'll be hard to explain to the cops how we found him and not explain how we got out."

"True. Even if you could explain Charming, you wouldn't want to explain the new port system that Milo is developing."

Liev smiled at her insights. The elevator vanished, and they walked to the apartment.

Lani noted the front door was now closed, reminding her. "Maybe you could show me how I can close this door and open it, from both the outside and the inside," she said. "While we did several trips in and out between the two apartments just now, we had to leave it open."

"*Hmm.*" Liev was focused on the front door. "The door is closed now. So presumably it closed automatically after the time-lapse control was triggered."

That made sense. As much as anything here did.

Liev shared a look with Milo; then he nodded to his

brother. Milo worked his wrist comp, and the door slid open.

Stepping inside, she watched as Liev secured the door behind her, then she opened her arms and collapsed against him. She hugged him tight. "Please, don't leave like that *ever* again."

He cuddled her close. "I'm not planning on it." He dropped a kiss on her forehead. "I think you need to sit down and relax."

"I'm thinking a nap in the healing pod might be a better idea. I'm seriously wiped out. Still not accustomed to the environment here."

"Good idea. You do that, and I'll start dissecting the information Milo stripped off Johan's communication center."

She walked to the pod room, calling behind her, "Was much information there?"

"Lots. But we don't really know what it all means yet."

"Right. I'll leave you to it then."

At the pod, she crawled inside and sighed as the humming started, lulling her to sleep.

LIEV WATCHED LANI as she slept. He let out a heavy sigh. She'd done so much with so little, and it looked to have completely wiped her out. And they were a long way from being safe. As long as she was in the healing pod though, he could work on the next step. "Milo, make sure the stealth is on in the pod room," he said as he walked into the kitchen. "She needs some downtime, and I want to make sure that she can't be found."

Charming pinned him with that look Liev was starting to hate. The look that said he was falling down on the job of taking care of Lani. Liev could hardly argue. Lani had been in nothing but trouble since Milo had snatched her up. And she'd been the one to save him in more ways than one. His relationships with women had been superficial in many ways. In all ways, if that was possible. Until Lani.

Nothing was superficial about his feelings for her.

"Hey, lover boy, I could use your help here."

Liev gave himself a mental headshake. "I'm here. What's up?"

"Look at this," Milo said. "It seems like whoever was monitoring Johan's presence at his place came from the Council."

"And that would only be if he was a prisoner out on bail."

"Normally, but we're dealing with a corrupt Council. So I've searched the databases and find no sign that Johan did time or has a criminal record of any kind anywhere."

"But it would begin to explain the secret life that Johan liked to live." Liev studied the square holograph, tons of images moving faster than his eyes could interpret. "What are the chances that Johan had a criminal record, and it was wiped?"

"The odds are pretty good. At least I'm inclined to think so. Considering he was as cagey as he was, his history is a little too clean for my liking."

"That's what I was afraid of. But why would the Council be onto him?"

"That's the million-dollar question."

Charming yawned. "Someone in the Council is bad."

Both Milo and Liev stared at him.

"We already know that," Milo stated.

Liev nodded. "But how do *you* know that, Charming?"

"Think about it." He rolled his eyes, as if speaking to peons instead of peers. "Johan's been reporting, willingly or unwillingly, to someone in the Council. Only someone with power could wipe Johan's criminal history clean. So someone in the Council is doing this for the benefit of the good for all or for the benefit of himself. Knowing people, I'd say he's doing it for himself."

"Listen to him." Milo snorted. "He's making sense."

Charming raised one long-haired eyebrow and peered down his short nose. "Of course I am."

"Besides"—Milo grinned—"I'm all for anything that makes the Council the bad guy."

"But there could be other answers. We have to keep an open mind." Although Liev couldn't think of one.

And it was galling to think a cat had seen it first. Liev added, "It won't be just any one Council member. It will be maybe all four of the senior members, covering for each other."

"Or the Council is keeping tabs on things they shouldn't be, making deals with criminals," Milo suggested. "Or blackmailing criminals into working for them."

Liev tilted his head back and stared at the ceiling, his thoughts a jumble. "If Johan's pod is the issue, then it affects us a lot. If this is something Johan was into by himself, then we are only involved at the edge. And that could mean we can stay quiet, and no one will know anything. We're just afraid someone would know something. But they might not know anything."

"The real questions are, how to find out who knows what, and then what do we do to protect ourselves."

Charming added under his breath, but loud enough for the others hear, "And our food."

"I'm locking down this material from Johan and keeping it in a deep dark hole where no one can find it."

Charming stared at him. "Except for you guys, right? It's not blackmail material, but it might keep someone off your back if they know you have this ace in the hole."

"Ace in the hole?" Milo asked curiously.

"An old phrase," Liev said absentmindedly. "An archaic one at that." He pulled out his comp. "The lockdown of Johan's apartment makes sense if the

Council was the one forcing Johan into collecting dirty information. We're presuming he was doing it for them, to a certain extent, enough to keep them happy, but he could have just as easily been keeping plenty back to screw with them."

Charming sat back. "I like that last part."

"So do I." Milo grinned. "So let's see what else I can find."

An alert sounded through the apartment, followed by a robotic voice saying, "Stephen Cavendish requests a call."

Milo looked up slowly. "Oh? Interesting."

"Yeah, let's see what he has to say." Liev flicked the buttons to open the communication system. Instantly Stephen's face and shoulders popped out of the Holo-Komp. "Good to see you, Stephen. What can I do for you?"

"Sorry, this isn't a social call. We have alerts coming from your building. A death and rodents."

Milo froze. He picked up Charming and walked him down the hallway to the pod room. Liev heard the door open and close. "Sorry to hear that. Anyone I know?"

"Johan Strand."

With what he hoped was a suitable look of shock, he said, "Johan? He's deceased?"

"Apparently. A Medivac team has been dispatched. Someone anonymously reported the death. But we have no idea who it was."

Liev raised his eyebrows. That alert had to have come from the intruder who escaped because Milo didn't send one with Johan dying suddenly. "I have no idea who that would be. I was under the impression that you were searching for Johan, but he was on the run."

"And apparently he returned and was living quietly under everyone's radar."

"What can I do to help?" Liev asked.

"I need to know everyone's whereabouts for the last four hours."

Liev narrowed his gaze and felt his temper simmer. Not to mention the fears arising as well. "Are we suspects in Johan's death too?" he asked incredulously.

"Not at all. However, the Council wants to clarify who reported Johan as deceased."

"Well, it wasn't me. Or Milo or my wife."

"There are signs that someone from your apartment accessed the rooftop from your elevator. Several times, in fact."

Liev tilted his head. "Yes, that's quite possible. My wife's cat got loose today when we were trying to fix the front door after Hahn's death. She had taken her cat up to the little rooftop garden a couple days ago, and she figured he might have gone up there again."

"I need to speak with her."

"And why is that?" Liev's voice deepened with anger. No way would he force Lani to speak to the Council. "Particularly when the documents are in place for me to speak on her behalf."

Chapter 9

LANI WOKE UP slowly. The heat from the pod was a welcome relief from her earlier stress. It felt like she'd slept for hours. Chances were good though that it was less than a half hour. She felt decent. With a yawn and a stretch, she pushed the pod lid open and swung her legs around. The room theme was still the Pacific island. She swore she could hear the surf as it rolled out in the distance. Could smell the flowers. Maybe they could leave and go to a Pacific island for real in a few days.

Or somewhere else. Anywhere else would be good. She needed a few days away. Milo and Liev could do with a break as well. Charming probably wouldn't care where they went, as long as food came with them.

She smiled at the thought of her baby. He slept, snoring gently beside her. He'd done so well getting in and out of Johan's apartment. He'd been quite the hero, saving the day. She hopped off the bed and wandered to the kitchen. Food and coffee were topmost on her mind. As soon as she'd imagined herself sitting on the island with a cup of coffee in hand, she'd been lost.

The kitchen appeared silent, until she made it around the corner and saw Liev in a discussion with someone on the HoloKomp. She didn't recognize the male holo image and had to remind herself that Liev ran a huge corporation that she knew nothing about. He interacted with hundreds of people. He had to get caught up on business sometime.

A pang of guilt hit her. He was behind because of her. Milo was busy doing something on the big 3-D monitor, both also appeared to have an ear tuned to the ongoing conversation.

That stopped her on the spot. She now tuned into the conversation too. And stopped herself from gasping, slapping a hand over her mouth. Milo grabbed her arm and tugged her to him. "Stay out of sight and be quiet."

She nodded mutely. "Did they find Johan?" she whispered.

"They know about his death. Presumably they will be sending someone to investigate further. They want to speak to you about what you saw."

Her eyes widened, and she shook her head. "Hell no." Then she winced. "Unless it helps you guys. I didn't really see anything."

Liev left the square on the floor, designated for HoloKomp conferences, to sidle up to his wife. "And, if you could tell them exactly that, I'd appreciate it," Liev said from beside her. "I've told them that you went up to the rooftop garden to search for your cat that got loose. It's not like you could see much from there, but if you could tell them the little bit you do know …"

He let his voice trail off and raised an eyebrow. She nodded. And took a step toward him. He held out his hand and drew them into the HoloKomp square. "Stephen, my wife, Lani."

Lani, suddenly shy, smiled. "Hello."

Stephen's face split into a broad grin. "Hi, Lani. Couldn't believe it when I heard this guy finally found the woman of his life."

Her smile brightened as Liev wrapped a possessive arm around her waist and pulled her close. "That I have."

"I'm sorry," she said, addressing Stephen. "I really didn't see much up on the roof. I wasn't focused on anything but my cat."

Stephen nodded. "Understood. But can you tell me if you saw anyone? Anything?"

"Oh, no. No one was up there. And the place was quiet." She opened her mouth to add that it was dead quiet and managed to choke back the words. But Stephen looked at her oddly, as if waiting for her to say more. Compelled to add something else, she said, "The place was locked down and silent."

"When you say, *locked down*, what do you mean?" Stephen asked curiously.

"It had steel doors all around. The other time I caught a glimpse of it, I saw a lot of glass everywhere. This time I couldn't see any glass."

Stephen frowned. "Interesting."

"It could have been just window coverings inside. It looked different from the last time I saw it."

"Thanks. I'm glad you found your cat."

Her smile this time was bright and happy. "Thank you. Me too." She stepped away from Liev, smiled at both of them, and said, "I'll leave you to your business."

"You're a lucky man, Liev," Stephen said.

Lani wanted to believe genuine admiration was in his voice, but she didn't know him. And everyone she'd met here so far had been less than what they had seemed.

She backed away and circled around to meet Milo. Charming had woke up and had joined them too. Bending close to Milo, she asked, "Was that all right?"

"Perfect." Milo reached forward and tapped the screen in front of him. "Look."

"What am I looking at? I can hardly see what you're pointing out with everything else going on." With every side of the monitor showing different images and all overlaying atop each other, it was confusing to see what he indicated.

Milo made several adjustments, and the monitors on three sides went black. In the center was a series of boxes with orange spots. "That's this building, isn't it?"

He smiled and nodded, then pointed to the spots around the middle of the building. "That's us."

How freaking fantastic was it that he could shift perspective like this? Then her gaze shot to the rooftop and the blacked-out apartment. Only it wasn't black any longer. An orange dot appeared ... on top. "And who is that?"

"We don't know."

"But you can find out?" She shot him a sideways look. "With the tags and visual stuff you guys do here, I'm sure you have it figured out."

"His tags appear to be undetectable, and he's wearing a mask."

"*Oooh*, interesting." She studied the spot. "Maybe he's just running something that interferes with the signal." Feeling Milo's sudden start, she glanced at him. "What? What did I say?"

"You could be right." He leaned his hands on the counter and stared at the display. "If he is running interference, then I should be able to bypass it." He frowned, then his fingers moved faster. "It could take some time though."

"Or don't bother. Wait until he leaves and track him then. Surely you can identify him from that point."

He snorted. "Say what?"

"Why try to bypass it? He had to arrive from somewhere. Can't you track him backward and check his tags from his earlier position?"

"Only I don't know which way he'll leave, and, if he ports out, then he'll disappear faster than I can track him."

She shrugged. "True. I thought maybe you gave him only one choice. But then all this is beyond me." She watched Liev end the conversation. The Holo-

Komp disappeared. She walked toward him, catching an odd look on Milo's face as she did so. She raised an eyebrow in question, but he shook his head. She reached Liev's side. "Is everything okay?"

"As good as it can be." He tugged her into his arms. "You look much better after your nap."

"I feel better." Her stomach grumbled. She gave a tiny laugh. "Sorry. It's been a while since I've eaten."

"I'm hungry too," Liev added. He turned her toward the kitchen, where his brother worked. Charming, awake and alert, watched them with hungry eyes. "Yes, Charming. I'm making a meal."

Charming flopped to his side and rolled over in ecstasy.

Liev laughed. "That's the closest I've seen you to looking happy in a long time."

"You haven't fed me in a long time either," he moaned. "*Food.*"

"Ha." Lani smiled. "Now you can be patient while Liev cooks."

"Shrimp would be good," Charming said, with a long-suffering groan of hunger.

"Cat food is what you're getting."

"That works." He sat up and proceeded to clean his paw.

Liev set about making a hot meal. He'd ordered

salmon earlier, thinking that might be the kind of meal Lani would love. He knew that Charming would if no else cared for it. Lani made coffee and watched him prep the fish.

When the meal was almost ready, she set the table, asking Milo, "Are you going to have a booster drink with us?"

He looked at her blankly. "Why?"

"So you can join us for the family meal."

He stared as if that were a foreign concept.

Liev grinned and smacked his kid brother lightly. "Yeah. Come join us."

"Not now. I'm on the hunt."

"Hunt for what?"

"This asshole."

"But you know where he is." Lani walked back over to the comp. "He's still showing up at Johan's place. So what's the big deal?"

"Hey, I'm just taking note of your suggestion and taking it one step further."

Liev looked up from plating dinner. "Really? What did she suggest?"

"To only give this guy one escape route, so we could ID him." He grinned, that boyish look Liev loved and hated at the same time. "I figured we'd use Johan's equipment to pick up anything we needed to know. Like this guy's comp number."

That didn't sound so bad. "And what good will that do?" Lani asked.

"If we can ID him, we'll figure out who he works for."

"Or not, considering the Defino brothers are still out there, and one of them is likely to be in Johan's apartment right now." Liev set the plates down. "Stephen is sending in a team."

"When?" Lani asked.

Milo laughed. "Right now from the looks of the orange spots shooting up to the rooftop. Looks like we'll get to see some fireworks soon."

"Except we can't see anything."

"Then come here and watch. I'll plug in the video."

And, sure enough, the inside of Johan's apartment showed on-screen.

And the intruder, dressed in black, paced back and forth.

CHAPTER 10

L ANI HATED THE suspense. They needed to know who was in Johan's apartment. And what that person might want from there. Lani was more concerned about what they might know about her—if anything—and what they would do with that information.

"Lani, come and eat."

She spun around, completely forgetting that Liev had cooked a meal. Then her stomach reminded her. With a last look at the comp, she took her place at the table. And couldn't stop staring at the scene unfolding on the screen.

"Milo."

"Yeah?" But his voice was distracted as he watched the screen.

"Bring it over here," Liev said. "Then we can all watch, without getting a kink in our necks."

Lani's attention was caught by his words. "Bring it over?"

And, sure enough, Milo arrived at the table, and suddenly the big 3-D monitor sat at the side of the table where they could all see. "I had no idea you could do that!" she exclaimed. "That's totally awesome."

Liev smiled. "It's fun seeing things from your perspective." He pointed to the see-through image. "We get blasé about our technology."

"You have no idea how much you've advanced." Her gaze was caught by the orange blobs surrounding the top apartment, with the intruder still inside. "And then, in some ways, nothing has changed."

"The criminals are more sophisticated, but they still exist."

"Crime is everywhere," Milo said. "Then again, what do you expect when the Council is corrupt as well?"

Lani lifted a forkful of hot food, then gasped as she watched the team enter, surround, and attack the intruder. He collapsed to the ground, and darned if that hot spot didn't slowly fade to yellow.

She put down her fork, suddenly sick to her stomach. "It was fascinating to watch—like a movie—but, at the same time, I just realized that a person died. It's not so nice now."

"And I'm glad to hear you say that," Liev said in between mouthfuls. "This monitor allows one to see what wouldn't normally be seen, while allowing the viewer to distance himself from the reality." He took another bite. "But it's not a vid. It's real life."

"Good thing it was a bad guy." Charming finally lifted his head from his bowl of food and proceeded to clean his face. "And this bad guy would have killed us."

"But we don't know that," Lani protested. "He might have been a nice guy and not out to hurt us."

All three males stared at her.

She sat back and sighed. "Okay, so that's not likely. But I don't want to be so complacent that someone's death is not a concern."

Liev reached across the table and grasped her hand. "That's not likely to happen."

"Good. Please remind me of this conversation later."

"I will." He gave her hand a squeeze and then released it to resume eating.

"I'll remind you too." Charming gave her a fat smirk.

"I can do without your input, thanks."

She polished off her dinner in silence, her gaze watching the rest of the drama in Johan's apartment play out. The team of orange blobs collected the injured intruder and were moving down the building—at a slower pace. "Surely they could move him out of there much faster?"

"Actually they could." Liev frowned. He got up and walked over to his wall comp. Lani watched the orange blobs stop about midlevel. She gasped. "Are they here?"

An alarm sounded.

LIEV HAD PLANNED to ask Stephen about the raid, …

when the alarm went off again in his apartment. He quickly told Lani and Charming to go to the pod room.

She had a puzzled look on her face, but she scooped up Charming as requested. At least she no longer panicked as she had earlier. Good. When she'd entered the pod room, he double-checked that stealth was on to keep her presence secret. Then he turned off the alarm to his front door and opened it.

ComBots. A robotic retrieval death team. Or, as some called them, … death squads.

"What can I do for you?"

"Identification required."

"I am Liev Blackburn."

"Acknowledged. We need this man identified." And a body bag was thrust forward.

Liev blanched. "Why me?"

"We need to know if you recognized him from the earlier altercation."

"Let me see his face."

He expected to have the body bag opened, but instead a tablet was shoved under his nose, a large image of a dead man on the screen. "That's Johan Strand."

"Thank you." And the ComBots retreated.

Liev stepped outside. "Wait. Who is in the bag?"

"You just identified him," the leader said.

"No," Liev snapped. "I did not. I identified the face on the tablet, not the body in the bag."

"Same man."

"No." He shook his head. No way in hell they were

the same man. He didn't know what was going on here, but they were trying to pull something, and he didn't want his identification of one dead man to be mistaken for the identification of another dead man. "I need to see his face."

"We cannot allow that."

"Then my identification does not stand."

"You have already identified him."

The ComBots were only computers. Advanced computers, but not conversationalists. "No. I identified the picture on the tablet. I need to see the face on the body in the bag to confirm."

"We can't allow that."

"Yes, you can. And I have Councilman Stephen Cavendish's permission."

The ComBots buzzed, as if forwarding the request to the Council.

"The Councilman cannot be reached."

"Well, he gave me permission." Liev walked closer. As much as he didn't want to look at any dead man's face in reality, he did want to know who was in the bag. The ComBot turned and conversed with another bot. Liev walked closer. He turned his back on the bots and quickly opened the bag.

"Stop. You cannot do this."

"Too late. I have done it." And it was not Johan. "This is Paul Defino. Older brother to Tommy Defino. This is not the man on the tablet. I repeat, this is not Johan Strand." He turned, anger building inside him.

"Where is Johan Strand's body?"

"We do not have it. This is the only body that we have collected."

"Why did you not collect the other one?"

"There was no other body to collect."

CHAPTER 11

L ANI HAD BARELY relaxed in the pod when Liev opened the door. "Lani?"

She poked her head out. "I'm awake. What's up?"

"That was a death squad of ComBots. They have one of the Defino brothers, bagged and tagged. Dead."

"So that's who was up there? Interesting."

"Even more interesting, Johan's body was not there, according to them. They, being robots, can be ordered to do one thing, then reprogrammed to forget what they did. But it appears that whoever is behind this is hiding Johan's death."

He walked closer and pushed open the pod lid higher so she could swing her legs around and hop off. "They are gone. I've been trying to reach Stephen, but there's no answer—anywhere."

She winced. "That always sounds so ominous. I was hoping that they'd caught the bad guy, collected poor Johan, and now we were safe."

"I'm hoping that's exactly what the situation is, but I can't be sure of anything at this time. It's almost bedtime, so maybe Stephen got word from the team and now has turned off his comp."

"I'm not sure I can sleep now." She walked with him down the hall to the living room. "I am tired but more wired. Wondering when this will all go away."

"I wonder what happened to Johan."

"Are you sure the death bots didn't remove his body?"

"They said they didn't. If they did, they didn't let me see it. I only saw one body bag, and that held Paul Defino." Liev slipped a hand up the nape of her neck and gently massaged the tight muscles. "I'm sorry there have been so many issues since you arrived."

"Apparently many were caused by my arrival." She moaned gently as he stopped, turned her around, and dug in his fingers to knead deeper. "Where's Milo?"

"Retired for the night."

Her insides perked up. She looked over her shoulder and gave Liev a fat smile. "So does that mean we are alone?"

"Not quite," Charming said. "But I'm heading in to lie beside the fire, so don't mind me."

She laughed. "We won't. Keep your ears shut."

"I'll sleep instead. Just don't wake me."

She watched as her baby sauntered toward the hallway into Liev's bedroom. That was where she wanted to go.

"He not only talks but thinks, has words of wisdom, and can solve puzzles," Liev said. "He's quite a puzzle himself."

When Charming had disappeared from sight, Lani

turned to face Liev. "Now are we alone?"

His smile quirked. "As alone as you want to be."

She ran her hands up his bare arms, loving the feel of his silky skin. "Good. And it's late. So …"

"So …?"

She raised her eyes to his. "Bedtime?"

"Absolutely." A slow smile quirked, lighting a fire in her heart. "Back to the pod or …"

"Or … your bed?"

He lowered his head and kissed her. "Definitely my bed."

In a move that shocked a surprised squeak out of her, he scooped her up as if she were no bigger than Charming.

Snuggling close, she yawned. "You live a crazy life."

"It's your life too." He walked toward his bedroom, nudging the door open with his foot. Sure enough, the fire burned bright. Overhead, the big timbers affixed to the ceiling sprawled the length of the room. She shook her head. "This is so amazing."

"Glad you like it. I can change it, if you'd rather have a different scene."

"No," she cried out. "This is perfect."

He walked over to the bed and softly dropped her in the middle of the big poofy comforter. She laughed. "I love this. It seems like forever since I spent a night in a bed."

"It has been forever." He turned away to lock the bedroom door, then glanced at the big plush rug in front of the fire, where Charming slept. "Charming, in or out?"

All they heard was a heavy guttural snore.

Lani added, "He'll be fine in here with us. He's a heavy sleeper."

"Good. Two's company in the bed, but three is a definite crowd."

"I'd get used to it if I were you. Charming has always slept in the bed with me."

"Not right now. This is the time for just the two of us." He walked to the side, and, while she missed what he'd done to make it happen, a large series of built-in shelves and hooks appeared, where he hung his clothes after stripping them off. She sat up, wondering what they did with laundry. "Do you have a laundry service, or do you wash your own clothes?"

He paused momentarily as he took off his wrist comp. His shoulders started to shake. He turned with a silly grin on his face. "Haven't you figured it out yet? We don't do menial work anymore."

Her mouth dropped open. "None?"

"None."

"You cooked," she accused. "And cleaned up."

"Did I?"

She stopped and had to think. No one had washed dishes. She'd assumed that Milo had cleared the table, but she hadn't seen that happen either. So really she had no idea. "You don't do laundry? Dishes?"

"No. I'll show you the kitchen cleanup tomorrow.

But I can show you the laundry process now. Hand me your clothing, and I'll hang them up. That's it. It will be clean and ready to wear again in the morning."

Her mouth gaped open. "That cupboard will wash your clothes?"

"It's like a mini dry-cleaning service inside." He stood completely nude in front of her, as unconscious of his nudity as she was conscious of it. Then again, she'd have to be dead to not notice. "Do you want to try it?"

"Oh, yes, please." Trying to be as natural stripping in front of him as he was with her, she stripped down to her skin and walked over. He showed her where to hang up her items. When done, he closed the closet and pushed a small button. "Do this every night, and every morning the clothes will be clean and ready to be worn. If you don't do it all the time, it stacks up, and you have to stand here and do this over and over again."

"Marvelous." Lani turned to him and smiled brightly. He opened his arms.

She stepped into them, loving that they instantly closed securely around her.

LIEV PULLED BACK slightly so he could look into her deep blue eyes. She was so beautiful. So natural that he couldn't imagine any enhancements that would improve what Mother Nature had given her. She wouldn't agree, but that he'd found was the way of women. Maybe people in general.

"What are you thinking?" she asked, a small shadow sliding into her gaze.

She didn't know him well enough to understand his actions, the nuances of his voice, yet she stood before him, as bare as the day she'd been brought into this world, with such trust, and he felt his heart swell. "I was thinking that I am the luckiest man alive." And damn if his voice didn't drop to a hoarse whisper. He closed his eyes and set his chin on top of her head as his emotions choked him. "I don't know why I am so blessed, but I truly am grateful that you are here in my life, in my arms tonight."

She snuggled closer, the brush of her nipples against his chest a sweet torment, the slide of her arms around his chest a delight. When she laid her head against his heart, he thought he'd cry. Instead, he crushed her against him and held her tight.

She deserved so much more. And he planned on giving it to her. He gently picked her up and carried her to the bed. In some weird sense of tradition, a night in his bed meant the start of their married life. A wedding night for just the two of them.

He flipped back the covers and lay beside her. Instantly she turned toward him. God, he loved it that she wanted to be here with him. Not just some party where everyone came to have fun with anyone, not because he was wealthy and eligible, but because she wanted to be here with him—because she cared.

Heat rolled through him. He needed that. Needed her.

Her hands slid up his chest to cup his face. He shuddered. "Are you all right?"

"Yes," he murmured. "Just a little overwhelmed."

"Same here." She kissed him gently. "I came a long way to find you, Liev."

He shuddered again, her words finding all the lonely places in his heart and filling them.

"I've missed you all these years," she whispered against his neck, her breath warming him to his toes. "Where were you, Liev?"

She dropped more kisses on his chin, then on his neck, before moving to his collarbone. A trail of heat, then ice followed as she drifted her way down his body. He wanted to tell her to stop. Wanted to pleasure her, but the words wouldn't come out. The need to be, to exist, as is, with her like this, … it was too strong.

She propped herself on one elbow, then pushed him from his side onto his back and slowly worked her way downward.

"Let me," he said in a low voice. "I want to make this special for you."

"Oh, it will be," she assured him, a tiny smile playing at the corner of her lips. She slid her hand down. "Besides, you promised me."

"Later," he said, but, when her hand closed around him, he cried out.

"This is my time," she murmured, dropping kisses down his chest and across his ribs. "My turn."

And then she found him with her mouth.

Liev thought he'd died. Lani's mouth was so wet, so sweet, and so damn hot, he almost couldn't hold on. He was afraid to move. Afraid she'd stop. And afraid she wouldn't. He didn't want this over too soon. She scraped her teeth down the long length of his shaft.

He lifted his hips and groaned.

Then her mouth was gone. He opened his eyes to find her carefully shifting over him, straddling his hips. She grasped him gently in one hand as she found her position.

And lowered herself.

His groan rumbled free. He couldn't help himself. He reached up and grabbed her hips to hold her steady, and he lunged upward, grinding his pelvis against her. She gasped and threw her head back, tightening her inner muscles.

He shuddered at the delicate internal massage. "Oh, God," he whispered. "Lani, you feel so freaking good."

She laughed, a wild abandoned sound that ended on a low moan. She leaned forward, dropped a tongue-dueling kiss on him, and started to ride.

He was a goner. In heat. In lust. In love.

And that no longer scared him. Emotion overwhelmed him. "Lani," he cried out.

"I'm here, Liev," she whispered. "Just let go."

"Not … without …" He flipped his head back and

forth, the tension coiling tighter and tighter. He didn't want to let go. He wanted this to last … forever. "Not without … *you*." And he couldn't hold back. His body exploded, his hands holding her hips in place as he ground as deep as he could go.

Through the haze in his mind, he heard her cry out, her thighs holding him tightly. He shuddered. When she collapsed on his chest, he held her close against his heart. "I think I'm in love."

She froze. Then a tiny giggle slipped free. "Only *think*? 'Cause I don't have any doubt."

He rolled over, still inside her, and pinned her underneath him. He stared down into her beautiful luminescent eyes, so full of joy, satisfaction, and, … yes, … love.

"Neither do I," he whispered. "I don't know how I got to be this lucky, but I love you, Lani. So very much."

And he proceeded to show her all over again.

Chapter 12

A LONG TIME later, warm and happy, Lani rolled over and cuddled up against Liev.

His strong arms wrapped around her and pulled her even closer. He kissed her forehead before dropping back in exhaustion.

Good. She'd worn him out too. She smirked.

"I heard that," Liev murmured against her hair.

"No, you didn't."

"I felt it."

"Now that's possible." She waited, wondering if she should ask.

But Liev, ever sensitive to her needs, asked first. "What's on your mind?"

She shifted so she lay, arms crossed on his chest, chin resting on top. Where she could look into his eyes. Where she could see the truth. In a serious voice, she asked, "Did you mean it?"

His eyebrows shot up in surprise, but his eyes warmed all the way through. Even as satiated as she was, her body quickened at the heat glowing from his heart.

"I meant it. All of it. All the way."

She closed her eyes. In spite of herself, a tear leaked from the corner of her eye. She swore she was done with the bawling, but the depth of the feelings in his voice? … Well, she didn't think anyone had ever cared for her like he did.

"Please, don't cry." He pulled her higher up on his chest so he could kiss the tear away. "I didn't mean to upset you."

"You could never upset me by telling me how much you care." She smiled, blinking rapidly to stop more tears from rolling down her cheeks. "I was just realizing how much I want this. How much I missed out on when all my friends had loving relationships, and I didn't."

"I feel the same way. I didn't want to be with everyone and yet no one. I wanted to find someone to love, someone who'd love me."

She made a face. "I hate to say it, but it looks like we owe Milo our thanks."

Liev laughed. A deep rumble rolled through him, making her sigh with delight. "That we do, but we won't tell him just yet."

He flipped her over, and she whispered, "Tell me again."

"How about I tell you *and* show you." He paused one moment, before adding, "I love you, Lani Blackburn."

And then he lowered his head and kissed her.

HOURS LATER, AN alarm shuddered through the apartment. Liev bolted from bed.

Lani woke up beside him, a cry on her lips.

"Alarm on low."

Instantly the sound stopped.

"Liev," Lani said, now that she could be heard, "what's going on?"

"Intruders."

She gasped, clutching the covers to her chest. "What?"

Liev bolted out the door, even as he hopped on one foot trying to get into his pants and calling behind him, "Grab Charming and hide in the pod room."

He couldn't stay to make sure she obeyed his orders. Milo was stumbling through the kitchen when he arrived. "Any idea who it is?"

"No." Milo yawned but brought up the security system. "I also don't know if it's building-wide or just us."

"Find out." Liev headed to the front door and his wall control panel. "The exterior is secure. I can see no breach anywhere." He called out to Milo, "I can't see what's triggered the alarm."

"Uh, Liev?"

"Yeah?"

"Can you come here?"

Exasperated, Liev gave the panel one final look, but

it didn't have anything new to offer. "Coming." He bolted to the kitchen. There was no sign of Lani along the way, so he hoped she'd hidden as he had instructed.

In the kitchen, he came to a skittering stop. Milo faced him, and so did Lani, who'd managed to get completely dressed. Behind them both stood the younger Defino brother, Tommy Defino.

"What the hell?" Liev approached slowly, his hands partially up. "How did you get in here, Tommy?"

Tommy glared, his lip curling. "You're not the only one who's good with technology. The world is full of geeks. Just not so full of guys who can get the job done." He smiled a too-shiny grin. "Like me."

"And what job is that?" Liev studied the man, looking for some weakness. The asshole was cocky, confident. In fact, he looked too damn confident. This wasn't the first time he'd broken into someone's house, even a high-tech one like his. But under that veneer was anger, fear, and maybe a hint … of … desperation.

And that made him dangerous.

"Besides, you didn't use technology to get in here. Our scans would have alerted us. So how else?" While he waited for an answer, he studied his brother's face. Milo kept rolling his eyes to the left. Liev casually checked out Lani's pinched face, then carried on to the counter, where Milo was motioning.

Lani snorted. "When I left the door open earlier. You snuck in then, didn't you?"

"Well I did, and left a device behind so I could get

in again when I wanted to, like now."

Damn. That made sense. The system had been off while Lani was outside rescuing him and Milo. This kid could have snuck in and found a place to hide his device until he found the best time to return.

And Tommy nodded and laughed. "You geeks seem to think you're so damn smart. Sometimes the easiest way is the best way to do something."

Milo made a sharp movement with his head. Liev saw the large 3-D computer was up and running. The hot spots showed who was where in the building. It took him a moment to realize that Johan's place was once again occupied.

"Your brother already died in this building," Liev said in an even tone. "Are you sure you should be here?"

Tommy narrowed his gaze. "Like hell he did." Tommy turned slightly to look at the shutdown HoloKomp center behind him, as if wanting to call his brother.

"I saw his body myself. The ComBot death squad retrieved him." Liev realized the kid didn't know. "I'm sorry."

"I don't believe you. He's on a job." Tommy shook his head. "He'll check in when he can."

"Except something went wrong." Liev would hate to hear news like that from a stranger. "Sorry."

"Like hell. Paul is good. Better than anyone I know. You're just messing with me." He snorted and waved something around.

Liev's gut clenched. Shit. The guy had a laser gun. With a wave of his hand, he could cut a person in half. Lani wouldn't have a hope of escaping. She didn't even know what it was. "What do you want?" Liev asked in a cold voice. He smiled at Lani to reassure her, but his mind raced. What the hell could he do to protect them all? He took a step forward.

"Whoa. That's close enough."

Milo made a sharp movement of his head again.

Liev glanced at the monitor screen. He studied the three figures in Johan's place, then motioned toward the moving images. "Those are the ones who killed your brother. Most likely another death squad ComBot looking for the information Johan has secreted away."

"What? Like hell." Tommy waved the gun around again and grabbed Lani's arm, pulling her back a step. Lani lost her balance, only righting herself at the last minute when he shoved her forward again.

"Leave her alone," Liev snapped, his voice hard. He clenched his fists.

"Or what?" Tommy sneered. "It's not like you can do anything. She's coming with me."

"Why?" He needed to keep the asshole answering questions. He had to find out where Lani was being taken, not that he'd let her leave. ... He just needed an opening.

"What about me?" Milo asked.

Liev was happy to have the distraction his little brother added to this confab. They had to stop Tommy from leaving with Lani.

"I don't know anything about you. Unless you're worth something, you get to die along with Liev here."

"So you know me," Liev interrupted, "but I don't know you. Interesting. I presume you took care of Gina?"

"What do you know about that bitch?"

"Only that she was a bitch," Milo said. He'd shifted closer to the monitor.

"That she was." Tommy pushed Milo slightly away. He fell toward the counter and pushed something on the monitor, a move so slight it was almost unnoticeable. Liev did notice. Milo had unlocked the computer system. What was he up to?

Charming sauntered into the kitchen.

Then the balance of power shifted.

Lani gasped. Liev watched, waiting with a fatalistic attitude, knowing that something was about to give.

Casually Charming hopped up on the counter by the monitor. He started to clean himself.

Like any ordinary cat.

"That is one ugly cat."

Uh-oh.

Charming froze. His whiskers quivered. He turned to stare at Tommy. In a low voice, he snarled, "What did you say?'

Liev groaned.

Lani rushed to talk. "Poor baby, you've still got that horrible hoarse voice." She rounded on Tommy. "How dare you say that about my cat?"

The poor guy's jaw worked. He frowned, his shocked gaze going from Lani to Charming and back again. "Did that cat just talk?"

"You're losing it." Milo laughed. "How can a cat talk? Get too many bangs on the head, by any chance?"

Tommy glared. "Shut the hell up."

Behind Milo, a series of weird beeps started.

"What's that? What did you do?" Tommy raced to the monitor, dragging Lani with him.

Charming scurried backward out of the way. Liev looked at him suspiciously. Charming gave him a bland look back. What the hell had he done?

Milo studied the computer. Liev caught a grin on his baby brother's face before Milo wiped his face clean. So Charming had done something good. Could they be so lucky?

"Turn it off," Tommy snapped. "Hurry up."

Milo reached over and tapped in a code. Instantly the unit silenced.

Tommy relaxed. "That's why you shouldn't have pets around computers. They'll fry the circuits."

"This one is particularly bad." Milo smiled. Charming snickered.

Tommy stared at Milo suspiciously before switching his gaze to Charming. "Should throw the damn thing out the window."

"You'd do that?" Lani rounded on him. "What kind of a horrible person are you? Animals are innocent.

They don't deserve that type of behavior." She poked her finger into his chest. "What kind of an asshole are you?"

"The asshole with the gun. Now lay off, lady." He spun around, his glare angry and frustrated. "What kind of a house is this?"

"A good one," Lani said with a sniff and lifted her nose. "Unlike the one you live in."

Tommy shook his head. "I don't know why the boss wants you. I wouldn't want to be anywhere close to you."

She deliberately stepped closer. "Yeah, how about this close?" She took another step. "Or this?"

"Stand back. I mean it."

Liev watched, fascinated, yet simultaneously worried as hell, as Lani, her temper up now, shoved her face into Tommy's. "Why should I? You can't hurt me. The boss paid you good money to make sure you don't. So are you going to defy your boss and hurt me?"

Tommy winced at the thought.

"Yeah, I didn't think so."

Liev wanted to wince too, because Lani wasn't thinking. Tommy could just as easily hurt them … or use Charming against her instead to get her cooperation.

As if reading Liev's mind, Tommy swung his arm out wide, bringing the laser gun around to bear on Charming.

And Charming jumped.

Chapter 13

CHARMING LANDED ON Tommy's arm. Claws dug in deep. Tommy screamed. And the laser gun went flying.

Milo jumped for the gun.

Liev jumped for Tommy.

Lani jumped for Charming.

"Get it off me," Tommy screamed, dancing backward, half bent over, and still shaking his arm. Liev pinned him against the counter, twisting Tommy's free arm up and behind him.

"Charming, let go." Lani tried to pull Charming off the man, but Charming was not interested. "Please, Charming. You'll get hurt."

"*He's* getting hurt?" Tommy screamed hysterically. "What about me? I'm the one who's been attacked."

Milo snickered. "Then you shouldn't have threatened Lani. The cat is very protective of her."

"You guys are nuts. Do you hear me? Bat shit crazy!" This last bit he delivered at the top of his lungs.

"Ha," Lani snapped. "You're the one who attacked a poor defenseless cat."

"What?" Tommy stared at her in shock. "I didn't

attack him. He attacked me. And that makes him anything but defenseless."

"Not the point. You insulted him first." With Charming now safe in her arms, she cuddled him close. "Ignore him, Charming. He's just being mean." Charming popped his head over her arm to glare at Tommy, and damned if he didn't stick his tongue out at him. She caught his move out of her peripheral vision and glared at Charming. He raised an eyebrow and pulled it back in.

"Did I just see that? Did you just see that?" Tommy cried out. "That cat stuck his tongue out at me."

"You really need to lay off those recreational supplements." Milo laughed. "Natural is fine but not in the doses you've been indulging."

"What are you talking about?" Tommy groaned. "You all belong in the nuthouse."

"Right, and you're the one making crazy talk about a cat," Liev snarled.

That shut him up.

Lani watched from a safe distance as Milo handed the gun off to Liev, who then held it on Tommy, as Milo checked over their intruder for weapons and communication devices. When Milo pulled Tommy's personal comp from his pocket, he stepped back and started clicking away on it.

"Hey, that's mine," Tommy protested. "Don't mess anything up."

Milo rolled his eyes at him. "He's got both Gina

and Hahn in his address book, and yes, here's Johan. Just like we found on Paul's comp.

"Hey, how did you get my brother's comp?"

"He conveniently left it behind here," Liev snapped, "when he broke in while we were dragged off to the Council."

"So that means nothing. Johan is behind all this bullshit."

"Then you're left holding the bag—in big trouble, kid—because Johan is dead, as is your brother, Paul," Liev said, his voice icy and hard.

Tommy froze. "What?"

"I said, Johan is dead. As is your brother."

"That can't be. No." Tommy shook his head. "Paul said to come here and to grab Lani. How Johan said she needed tags. And we know what that means. Paul had an argument with Johan about it, when Paul tried to retrieve the information for the Council. Johan wouldn't tell Paul where the info was. Only someone else was there. Paul barely escaped that time, so he had to go back."

"That argument finished Johan," Liev stated with some heat. "He'd been hurt before. Your brother must have given him the final blow to his injured body. So the Council did away with Paul for his failure to keep Johan alive long enough to find the information the Council wanted and then for not getting that data on his own." Liev paused, glaring at Tommy. "As far as the others in Johan's apartment, *we* were the others in that damn apartment. Your brother escaped from *me*," Liev snapped. "And, no, I don't know what *needing tags* mean. What does it mean?"

Tommy shook his head, trying to absorb the facts as they flew at him. "It means that she's not from here."

"So, she's from somewhere else," Milo said. "What's the big deal?"

"They are eradicating the fringe groups. You know that."

"No," Liev corrected. "The Council is isolating the fringe groups to live in one area, where they can't cause as much trouble."

"Talk about naive." Tommy snorted. "Look. They just dispatched a large group of them a few months back. When the alert came through on the tagging for Lani, they figured she'd escaped. She'd cause them a ton of damage if she spread the word."

Lani stared. "Are you saying someone committed mass murder, and they think I got away? And now I'm going to blow the whistle on them?" Oh, this was not good. Like, so not good.

"Who did this?" Liev asked Tommy in a hard voice.

But Milo answered, "The Council, of course."

And Tommy nodded. "They did. And they can't have anyone know what they did."

"Why kill these fringe groups? Were they terrorists?" Liev asked.

"That's what the Council will try to convince everyone," Tommy explained, "but they weren't. They were people who didn't want to live under the Council rule. They lived a more natural life."

Instantly Lani felt a connection to them. "Those poor men."

"Women and children too," Tommy added. "The Council was especially clear about making sure the breeding stock was taken out, so the problem couldn't continue."

Lani burrowed her face into Charming's lush fur. How terrible. Centuries in the future and genocide was still a problem. In her own country yet. She didn't know what to say.

Liev did. "Do you have any proof?"

"Johan had it. He was trying to make a break from being under their thumb. They blackmailed him into monitoring everyone." Tommy nodded at Liev and then at Milo. "Like you two. He didn't want to tell them about Lani here, but they saw the information from his pod, and they found out anyway."

LIEV HATED THE ring of truth in Tommy's words. This explained so much. Tommy no longer looked like a major badass. Instead, he looked like a punk who had made a wrong turn and didn't know how to make the right one to get the hell out.

Liev took a look at Lani. How was she taking this revelation? True to form, she had tears collecting in the corner of her eyes. He just didn't know why. Fear? Agony for the victims? Something else?

"That's a horrible thing to do," she said in a harsh whisper. "Those people just wanted to live their life their way."

Tommy nodded. "I agree. But you're dead meat regardless. The council can't afford to let you live."

Liev realized that Tommy believed Lani had escaped the massacre, and—if he did—others would too. She was marked. Unless this was resolved, ... and fast, ... there'd be no end to this hunt. Ever.

Except they had Johan's material. He spun around to look at Milo.

And his kid brother—as usual—was way ahead of him.

"You do realize the Council killed your brother?" Liev asked Tommy. "They couldn't leave him alive with what he knew about the genocide. They've already—or someone has—killed Gina, Hahn, Johan, and now your brother."

Grief filled the young man's eyes. "I was hoping you were lying. I haven't heard from Paul since last night. He was on a retrieval mission at Johan's."

"Retrieving what? The info on Lani?"

Tommy shook his head. "They had the pod scan on Lani, from Johan's pod, but it was too corrupted. That's why they need Lani in person, to run their own scans. But the Council knew Johan had something else. The data Johan had on the Council."

It all made such terrible sense. "And what will they do with you, now that you've failed?" Liev asked in a gentle voice. He wondered who had beaten Johan so well that he was inches away from death. Then again, thugs were easy to find and even easier to hire. It could have been one of many. All hired by the Council. Or rather, all blackmailed by the Council. Liev doubted Tommy knew about any of those "contractors," outside of his brother.

Tommy shook his head and said in a gloomy voice, "I'm dead already. The final act just hasn't happened yet."

Milo turned to look at him. "Run. Surely you can find a place to go where you can be safe."

Not likely, but Liev waited for Tommy's answer.

"No. I have no place to run to. All the Councils are connected. I could go to the other side of the planet, and they'd find me within a day."

"Unless we find a way to stop them first," Milo said.

Tommy looked up at Milo, a tiny bright bit of hope in his eyes. "What good would that do? You'll just throw me to them anyway."

"Did you kill anyone?" Lani asked out of the blue.

"Me? No." He looked shocked at the suggestion. "I'm good with computers." He shrugged. "I've committed many a break-in though. That will get me off-planet jail for life. And it's not fair. We were ditched early in life by Mum and had to fend for ourselves afterward. A little hard to do and to stay honest when you're trying to stay out of the system and have no family to turn to."

Liev nodded. And that was the biggest issue. No family to take them in and to give them a home. Without it, life could be a little grim. Hell, a lot grim.

Tommy confronted them. "So what will you do to me?"

Chapter 14

L ANI HEARD THE challenge in Tommy's voice. She carefully placed Charming on the table with a whispered warning, "Be quiet." He shot her a hooded look. She wasn't sure what he meant by that. She wanted to believe he'd be good, but there was no guarantee.

Ever.

Not with Charming.

Giving him a stern look, she walked over to Liev and slipped her hand into his. He squeezed her hand and tugged her up close. She murmured, "What can you do, Liev?"

"I'm working on it," he said with light humor. "Give me a minute."

She watched Tommy shift uneasily. Milo was back at the big computer. Now that Tommy had been disarmed, he'd lost his bravado. He just looked sad. Worn out. "How good are you?"

"At what?" He looked confused.

She glanced at Milo, whose face had twisted in thought. "Milo?"

"I'm thinking."

She groaned. "Could you two think a little faster please?"

"What difference does it make?" Tommy slouched against the back counter. "There is no going back for me."

She wanted the brothers to step up and to give the kid a break, but she didn't know enough of how life worked here to make that happen. Maybe the kid was a major badass and needed to be slung out onto some horrific planet all alone. What did she know? "Liev, can you help him?"

He glared down at her. "And why would I want to do that? He broke into my house and tried to kidnap you, besides threatening to kill me and Milo, not to forget about tossing Charming out of a window sixty floors up. Where in any of that does it say he deserves my help?"

"Because he didn't succeed, and he really had no choice himself."

"But he did in the beginning," Liev argued, his jaw stiff with anger.

"Did he?" She waited. She didn't know Liev as much as she'd like to, but she knew him better than he thought. He was a good man. With a good heart. A ruthless businessman, yes, but not at the expense of endangering people. He'd help Tommy if he could. If he saw a reason to.

"Oh no." He shook his head. "I know that look. No. We're not saving the world."

"I didn't ask you to save the world. Just one small part of it." She widened her gaze at him. "We couldn't save those on the fringe."

He closed his eyes and groaned. "Really? You're going there?"

She smiled. Milo laughed, then said, "She has a point."

Liev shook his head. "No. No, she doesn't."

"He's good," Milo said quietly, with a head tilt toward Tommy. "We could use him."

"Is he?" Lani asked, her hopeful gaze on Milo's features. He nodded. She switched her attention to Tommy. He was slumped with apparent disinterest, like he'd never known there to be anything but a bad outcome in his life.

"It doesn't matter how good he is, when he can't be trusted." Liev's hard voice brooked no argument.

But Lani had to admit to feeling perverse. "How do you know that? I imagine loyalty and trustworthiness are the two main requirements in Tommy's life up to now." She turned toward the very confused man, staring at her like she'd lost her marbles. "Or am I wrong?"

"No," he said in a rush. "You're not. They mean everything. Or I'd be dead by now."

She nodded, facing Liev now. "See?"

"No," Liev said in exasperation. "I don't see." He raised both hands in frustration. "He's a criminal. I can't change his history. The law wants him. The law will get him."

"I actually did my time. It's my brother who's ... was ... wanted by the law. Then the Council said I hadn't done all my time. Only I did. But because they said I hadn't ..."

"Juvie?" Milo asked, busy clicking away on his damn computer again.

Lani didn't know if he was helping the situation or playing games, but she wanted someone to do something. "Milo?"

"Yeah," he answered, distracted.

"What are you doing?" she asked.

"Looking at his record."

Tommy started. "You aren't supposed to be able to see that."

Milo snorted. "I'll look at whatever the hell I want to."

Tommy stared from one person to the other. When it was Lani's turn, she gave him a bright smile.

"Milo?" Liev waited for a response from his brother.

"Says he did his time. Was released four years ago. Model prisoner. Time off for good behavior."

"And they said that was revoked because I moved back in with my brother, who was a known criminal."

"That's not fair," Lani cried out. "You paid your debt to society. And he was family."

Tommy shrugged. "The Council said it wasn't enough. It's not like I can argue. They have all the power."

"Too much power apparently." Lani twisted slightly to face Milo and Liev. "Can you help him?"

Milo grinned. "I don't think Liev wants to. Tommy here was all set to screw with us. You in particular."

"Only because I had to." But he stared at Lani in fascination. "I've never met anyone like you."

"Not going to either." Milo almost danced in place with his secret.

But that was one secret that could never be shared.

LIEV STUDIED THE awkward young man in front of him. He wanted to slug him and hug him, for all that he'd tried to do. Liev couldn't help comparing Milo to Tommy. If Milo and Liev hadn't had the benefit of their extended family, where would they have ended up?

Likely the same damn place as Tommy. Considering Milo's seriously scary computer skills, they could be running the underworld by now. That brought a tiny smile to his face.

But that didn't change the fact that Tommy was dangerous. And alone in the world. "Tommy, how old are you?" Liev asked him.

The younger man's eyes narrowed. "Twenty-two. Why?"

Of course he was the same age as Milo, and Paul, his older brother, would likely have been about the same age as Liev. With Paul dead, Tommy was completely alone. But that didn't make him someone worth rehabilitating. Paul, his brother, had been a hard case. Several steps further down the crime path than Tommy. Was it too late for him to be saved?

Lani shifted patiently at his side, and Liev realized he really wouldn't have much choice, now that Lani and Milo had aligned their positions regarding Tommy. "He'd have to give over all the information he knows, sign a contract as to what he would honor, and should he break that contract ..." Liev deliberately added an edge to his voice.

Tommy's eyes lit up. "I'm not sure what you're talking about here as an end result, but I'm sure looking for a way not to go back to jail or to have to face the bosses."

"And just who are the bosses?"

He swallowed. Looked from one to the other. "Paul dealt with him. *Them.*"

"But you know who the bosses are, right?"

"They are all on the Council. But one is handling this Lani issue. He's the one we dealt with."

"Who? And is he the one who killed Gina?"

He winced. "We think so. But I don't know who he is. Besides, he commands many contractors. We were supposed to snatch Lani here, but, when we couldn't, Gina was blamed. Then they put the pressure on her partner."

"Hahn Driscoll, the attorney. Who came here to

grab Lani himself after Johan had bailed?"

"Yeah, the bosses want her bad."

"Alive?"

Tommy nodded his head vigorously. "They need to know who escaped with her."

"Right. And would torture the information out of her if necessary." Shit.

CHAPTER 15

L ANI MADE COFFEE again. Tommy was hardly a visitor, but the males sat at the table, discussing what was to be done, and would likely appreciate the coffee. And she had quickly become addicted to the stuff herself. Tommy was dishing dirt on everyone he knew in an effort to show his good intentions to clear himself. She felt sorry for him. He'd had it rough. He'd done the best he could, but now he was at a crossroads.

What he did from here on out would be dangerous and would change the course of his life. With his permission, Milo had run every kind of scan he could on Tommy while everyone had watched. And Milo had fixed some kind of emotion detector on the poor guy too. Lani felt horrible about that one. The last thing she would want was to have her emotions scanned or detected.

That Liev had never mentioned such a thing to her hopefully meant that he had trusted her at least that much from the very beginning.

"What's the matter?" Liev spoke quietly behind her. "Do all the tests we're putting him through bother you?"

"Yes," she said with feeling. "Especially the emotion one."

"We have to make sure he's telling the truth. Our lives depend on it."

She nodded. "I understand. I hope you guys never feel you need to do that to me though."

He laughed and tugged her against him. "Never. You're honest all the way through." His chest rumbled behind her head. "Besides, that's one of the tests Milo already checked you on before he chose you."

She stilled. "Really? How? I wasn't even here yet. Even so, how could he know for sure?"

"We have much more sophisticated ways to detect stuff like that now," he said easily. "Honesty is big for Milo. And, being in business, for me, it's even bigger."

"Me too," she said with feeling. "Particularly after your blackhearted ancestor."

He dropped a kiss on her head.

"What's to be done with Tommy?" she asked.

"I can't say for sure. Depends on whether we can catch the Council with what they are doing and stop them, or if we have to go on the run."

She tilted up her head. "Really? The latter sounds horrible."

"I am hoping that won't be necessary. The trouble is finding the information, then going above the Council to get them charged with criminal behavior, as well as letting the public know. Above the Council are only a few older men. They are supposed to be the watchdogs over the Council. But are they really?" Liev shrugged. "We won't know until we get to that point."

"Doesn't Milo already have that incriminating information?"

"Milo grabbed everything he could off Johan's system, but that doesn't mean he'd recognize the information when he sees it. I'd expect Johan to have it secured and barely identifiable. The material is too dangerous."

That made sense. "So is Tommy going to help Milo look for it?"

"Something like that. We know the material is encrypted. And breaking that encryption is likely to be the toughest part. Apparently Tommy's skills have to do with code breaking. That's how he and his brother have been so good with breaking into houses. Tommy manages to bypass security codes easily, letting Paul gain entry, like he did here to find the pod room and you and Charming."

She smiled. "Sounds like Milo has found a kindred spirit."

Liev dropped another kiss on her head. "The biggest issue is, do we trust him?"

"No. Don't do that at this point. Yet he's got a lot of reasons to expose the Council himself."

"And that's partly why we're running the tests."

"If he holds up his end of this, and we do expose the Council, what about Tommy then?"

Liev shrugged. "I don't know. Maybe if we get a

new Council, they will give him a medal. They'd certainly look at his criminal past with a more judicial eye than the current Council. He's being blackmailed into following their illegal orders now."

"Hopefully he'll come out fine."

"Chances are good." Liev looked over at Milo and Tommy, their heads together as they looked at the huge holographic monitor. Liev looked like he wanted to say something but stopped.

She nudged him. "What?"

He smiled down at her. "I'm not making any promises, but, if Tommy's any good, we could probably use him in the company. *Keep your friends close and your enemies closer* type of thing."

"So find the information. Blast it out to the world so everyone knows what the Council did. Make sure it can never be buried as yet another bureaucratic secret. And we need to tell someone about the Council's involvement in Gina's and Paul's and Johan's murders, but who?"

"I'm debating talking to Stephen."

"Your friend on the Council?" At his nod, she coughed lightly and said, "How can you know for sure that he's not a part of this?"

Liev's face scrunched. "I can't. That's why I'm still thinking about it. I don't want him to be involved, but who knows if everyone is or if it's only the four top-tier members."

Tommy twisted around to look at them. "I

wouldn't trust anyone on the Council. They're all privy to what goes on there."

"But Stephen is new. He hasn't even gotten full status there yet."

"He's too close to the top to be trusted. His meteoric climb within the Council makes me suspicious."

"You think he's been handpicked to climb that hierarchy because of his involvement in the corruption?"

Milo piped up. "Everyone in the Council will be involved. There's no way not to be."

"Except they need a fall guy," Tommy said. "What better way than to blame the new guy?"

"Or what better way for the new guy to cement his position than to arrange for the deaths of those interfering with the Council's plans?" Lani asked.

"There is that." Liev glared down at the huge computer. "How can we find out who is involved and who is not?"

LIEV HOPED STEPHEN wasn't involved. This was too important a mistake to make. He walked closer to Milo. "Any progress?"

"A little. I think we found the files, but Johan's layered it with different encryption techniques. We're still working our way in."

"Okay, I'll make some phone calls." Liev hesitated, still thinking. "See if there's anything I can find out on

Stephen's history."

"You're probably better off checking the government files," Milo told Liev, "and scanning them to see if they've been doctored."

Tommy stared up at Liev. "You guys can do that?"

"Sure," Liev said. "We're just not supposed to."

Instead of calling a few people he knew, Liev walked up to the computer on the kitchen counter. Everything looked normal in the building, and Johan's apartment was once again empty and dark. Liev might need to make a trip up there, just to see if the latest round of ComBots had discovered the cloaked high-tech room and computers and had somehow accessed them or carted them off.

He bored into the government database and did a quick sweep of Stephen's files. Liev scanned the information. Everything confirmed what he already knew about Stephen. It wasn't surprising. Liev had gone to business school with Stephen, and, even then, he'd been full of political idealism. Liev had been the opposite. He'd been full of commercialism and was all about protecting Milo and his inventions.

Stephen's records were all just as Liev thought, but this was surface stuff. Lani would expect him to do more. Damn it, he wanted to prove that Stephen was okay. Beyond any doubt. So Liev kept digging, using Stephen's middle name too. Nothing unusual in any direction. No leads and no red flags, which was to be expected. Stephen would be covering his tracks professionally, if he was involved in anything wrong. He'd been active in a few political rallies as a young man, nothing to raise eyebrows over, just enough to make him "normal." ... And that's what bothered Liev. On second glance, his buddy looked a little *too* normal.

Scowling, he went deeper.

And suddenly things got interesting.

Lani walked over and handed him a cup of coffee. He'd forgotten she'd even made it. He smiled his thanks.

"Did you find anything?" she asked.

"Maybe." Liev rubbed his eyes. "Signs that he might have had his fingers in a few gambling pots I hadn't known about."

"Bad pots?" she asked. "Or just a little recreational gambling?"

"A lot of money lost." He kept reading the information on the screen. "A hell of a lot of money lost."

"Maybe he had to replace it? And the Council offered him a way to do that?"

"Or they used his gambling debts against him?"

"Or they put that into his file to keep him compliant. He's in good financial standing everywhere else and his credits are excellent so no red flags there."

CHAPTER 16

"To make him go along with their plans? That could be possible." Lani didn't know the man, but it would be nice to think that not everyone here was an asshole.

The HoloKomp beeped. Liev walked over to stand in the weird square on the floor that tied in any visuals and audio into a holocall. Lani watched from a safe distance as Stephen's face came through the wall. From the corner of her eye, she caught Tommy's shrinking motion. Interesting. She flipped back to Liev, who seemed to be carrying on an animated conversation in silence. He must have muted the audio.

She turned around with raised eyebrows. Milo said, "Stephen has the conversation on double security levels."

"So it's serious." She sat down beside them. She leaned toward Milo and whispered, "Can you lip read?" He grinned and held up a finger to his lips, then tapped his ear. She realized that he was listening in on the conversation anyway.

Smart boy.

Standing, she walked to the table where she'd

placed Charming. He'd long since disappeared, but she was hoping he was close by. He wasn't. She went to the pod room, but there was no sign of him. Remembering the beautiful fire he so loved, she headed toward Liev's bedroom. Her bedroom now, she supposed, only it didn't quite feel like it yet.

"Charming, you in here?"

"Over here."

She turned to find him balancing on his rear legs on the back of a chair, his front paws on the wall, studying the wall computer there. She understood today was all about the technical age, but literally a built-in computer was in each room. She'd never seen what this one could do, but, since it was in Liev's bedroom, she doubted it did less than any other one in this apartment. In fact, as Charming spiked out a long claw and touched another part of the screen, she realized this one was similar to the one in the kitchen counter. Maybe they were all the same, and she only saw parts of them.

She asked Charming about that.

"Yes, they are all part of the same computer. You can pull out a section to look at via holograph at any place. They all have the same capabilities."

"And what are you doing?" She tried to see for herself, intrigued by the different screen loads he had open.

He said, "I'm looking for a list of those killed in the ongoing genocides of the Naturals."

"Why?"

"Because maybe it will give us some idea of who is

behind this."

"You think someone did this to their own people?" She shuddered. "That's a terrible thought."

"And yet your species seem to delight in finding ways to hurt each other even more."

"I was hoping that the future would be more developed," she muttered.

"It is, but people appear to be more stupid."

She had to admit, from what she'd seen so far, Charming wasn't far from wrong.

A long list appeared on the screen. "Any names we recognize?"

"Not yet."

The list scrolled on endlessly. She hated to think of so many people killed over the years, simply for being different. It was nothing new, but seeing the names of all those people brought tears to her eyes.

Suddenly Charming reached out and snagged the screen.

It stopped, and one name enlarged, supersize.

Stephen Cavendish.

LIEV HAD JUST closed the HoloKomp when Lani dashed around the corner of the kitchen. "Liev, come into the bedroom, please."

He raised an eyebrow, shrugged at Milo and Tommy, and followed her. Once inside, she closed the door so he could see the computer better. And what Charming had highlighted.

Liev swore under his breath. "It has to be a different Stephen."

"Does it?"

"It says he's deceased."

"How hard is that to fake?" Lani asked.

"To fake a death? Hard, but not impossible. Taking over someone's life? That's much easier to do."

"And the only reason to do that is to hide who he really is." Lani studied his face. "You're thinking he might have had something to do with the genocide and is now hiding?"

"I'm not thinking anything," Liev protested. "Okay, I'm thinking plenty of things. I'm trying to figure this out. Like, maybe this is a relative of Stephen's. There are too many unknowns."

"Then we need to make them knowns," she said. "What does your gut tell you about Stephen?"

Liev shook his head, his mouth set in a firm line. "I do trust him. I did anyway. I have trusted him all along. He's saved me and Milo several times while we stood before the Council. Maybe he did so many other times without us even knowing about it."

"So," Lani said, "you only have doubts now that you have dug this stuff up?"

Liev nodded.

"Then invite Stephen here and just ask him in private."

"That's not happening. Councilmen don't just travel around casually. They come with full ComBot units."

"Then figure out how to get him to come alone or to meet him elsewhere—just the two of you—so you can find out the truth. But stay safe too. It seems like he's at the center of this."

"And yet this deceased Natural might be a completely different Stephen Cavendish, not even related."

"Same birthday," Charming announced. "But everything else looks different."

"It would have been changed to hide his history," Liev muttered.

"So ..." Lani nudged him.

He ran his fingers through his hair. "I definitely need to talk to him. I'm just not sure how."

"I suggest you send him an encrypted message saying, 'I know everything,'" Charming said, "And have him meet you somewhere private but secure."

Liev stared at Charming. "For a cat, you're damn smart."

"Only because of Milo," Lani said absentmindedly. "And you're not going alone. Take Tommy to watch your back and Milo to make sure Tommy is actually watching and not stabbing you in the back."

He snorted, then admitted, "I hate the idea of leaving you alone."

"We're better off here," she said with a sweet smile. "All hell breaks loose when I leave." She reached out a hand and stroked his forearm. "Better you go, deal with this, and come back."

"Then I'd better get it set up now." And he headed out to join Milo and Tommy.

It was the last thing he wanted to do. But, if his friend was involved in this mess, then Stephen was in for an ugly surprise.

Friends or not, if Stephen was involved in Lani's kidnapping, Liev would fry him.

CHAPTER 17

I T WAS OUT of Lani's hands now, and she watched as everything happened in front of her eyes. After Milo encrypted the message, using a dialogue code common among the Naturals group, Liev sent it off.

They hadn't had time to prepare for the next stage when an answer came immediately.

Meet at Station 42, Zone 6.

Milo immediately searched for that location. "Interesting. It's an old hangout for the Naturals before they moved out. It's deserted and hasn't been used in decades."

Tommy shook his head. "That's what the records say, but it's not empty. A heavy criminal element is there."

"Then don't go," Lani cried out, facing Liev. "I don't want you to get hurt."

"We don't have much choice."

"Yes, you do," she argued. "You don't have to go to that location. Change it to someplace safer. One where these two can be with you. And one where you will all be safe."

Milo said, "She's right, you know?"

"Make it a public place," she said. "An art gallery? A huge shopping complex."

The men looked at her. She rolled her eyes. "Okay, so I like reading about places like that, but think of something along the same line. Or ..." She smiled. "Both of you port where no one can find you. Go to a ski chalet, where you can be alone and talk."

Milo brightened. "I like that idea. Give him the co-ordinates—a set he can look up—then we'll meet him there."

Tommy got up and walked over to the window. As he passed Lani, she saw pain and grief in his face, and she felt for him. He'd just lost his brother, and now his life had taken a complete shift. Adjusting would be hard.

"Why not just send him to Johan's place?" Charming asked from behind Lani.

Lani quickly glanced at Tommy, to see if he had heard her cat talking out loud, but he was staring out the window, his back hunched. She turned to the others. Thankfully, Tommy was far enough away, and maybe too engrossed in his grief, that he couldn't hear Charming talking.

Milo turned to Liev. "That's an even better idea. We can track you, and everything can easily be record-ed."

"And we can help from here." Lani loved the idea of Liev staying close.

Liev nodded. "That's the best plan yet."

"Then send him an updated message and get the meeting place changed," Lani urged. "At least Charming and I can keep watch from here and help out if need be."

Milo added, "Remember. We don't know if Stephen is on the good side or the bad."

"True," Lani said, "but he responded—and damn fast—so he's interested."

Milo walked out of the room and returned a few minutes later with a cloud of tiny colorful dots in his hand. "Here. Swallow."

Lani watched with interest. That Liev swallowed the items without asking questions said a lot about them. Tommy had turned around, and even he didn't raise an eyebrow. So this was a common occurrence. She assumed they were trackers of some kind. Knowing Milo though, it could be so much more.

She sat in the background, as messages were fired off and as Milo prepped his brother and Tommy. "Tommy and I will be going up there earlier and will be in the spare bedroom under Johan's camouflage. I'll bring my new invention, and I'm setting up a smaller one for you to take as well, Liev. In case of trouble, it will be best for all of us to have an escape route."

"I hear that," Tommy said.

Lani loved how Tommy had gone from being a bad guy to a good guy. She just hoped he didn't blow this second chance. The Blackburn brothers would help him, but, if he screwed up, ... Liev would kill him.

Hell, she would too. Lani shifted restlessly.

"*Psst.*"

Damn, that was Charming. She walked to the bedroom and closed the door. "What?"

"Make sure Milo sets up that emotion scanner for Stephen. Might help see what the truth is."

"Oh, good idea. But I don't think it's portable."

Charming snorted. "Hell, everything is portable here."

She glanced down at her beloved cat. "Charming, you look tired."

"Of course I'm tired. It's not like there's any chance to catch up on all our lost sleep."

"I hear you there." She yawned unexpectedly. "I'm really tired too."

"So let's go for a nap." Charming's gaze brightened. "They can go do their super-secret spy stuff, and we can sleep."

"But someone has to keep an eye out to make sure Liev is safe."

"Ha. He's willingly going into that locked-down prison called Johan's apartment. If he screws up, I'm not going back in there after him."

"You won't need to. Milo is taking that portable-port thingy you delivered last time."

"Good. Nice to know I won't be called on to save the day again. Being a hero is tiring." He pinned her with a glare. "And works up an appetite. I'm feeling better, but you're really slacking in the meal department."

"Hey, no one else is complaining of hunger."

"My stomach tells me it's time for breakfast. Besides, it's breakfast or lunchtime or dinnertime somewhere in the world."

"Lani?" Liev gently pushed the bedroom door open. "Stephen has agreed to the new location. Milo and I are going up there now to set up. Are you going to be okay here?"

Charming glared at him. "We'll be fine if you'd let us sleep."

Lani shook her head. "Don't mind him. He gets cranky without his beauty rest." She smiled brightly at Liev, feeling anything but on the inside. "We'll be fine, but what about Tommy? And what do we do if things go bad?"

"I was thinking about leaving Tommy here in that case." He tugged her into his arms.

She wrapped her arms around his waist and whispered, "I don't want anything to happen to you."

"Ditto. But I also want a life where we don't have to worry about anyone else coming after us. Looking over our shoulders all the time will not be fun."

"Can you take Tommy with you and leave Milo here?" She bent back to look up at him. "Or send Milo back right away and make them switch places?"

"That's possible. I'll talk to Milo."

"Also Charming suggested running that emotion scanner on Stephen."

Liev nodded, smiling at them both. "Milo's got it ready to go."

AND TALK TO Milo he did. Inside, outside, upside, and downside, and his kid brother still wouldn't budge.

"I'm not leaving you up there," Milo snapped. "No way."

"What about Lani?"

"You're my brother. It's your back I'm watching."

"And, as your brother," Liev said, concern for Lani a hard lump in his throat, "I'm asking you to come back and look after Lani."

Milo shook his head, the huge mohawk wafting in the wind. "No. I'll make sure you are safe so *you* can look after her. That's the best thing I can do for both of you."

And that was his final word.

Tommy butted in. "Look. I understand that you don't know me." He paused and winced at the looks from Liev and Milo. "But I do have some experience with this brother stuff."

Now that much was true. Liev could hear the sorrow in his voice and could see it in the way he swallowed before continuing.

"I get that you can't fully trust me yet, and we didn't have a good start, but you have your tests and scans to know that I'm telling you the truth when I say that I mean you and Lani no harm. I want to find out who is behind all this and to stop it." He took a deep breath and added, "I'd like my life back."

Liev glanced at Milo, who was studying the comp screen in his hand. Milo looked up and nodded. Meaning Tommy was being honest. That helped, but this was the worst time to be wrong.

Still, it's not as if Liev had much choice here. His kid brother who had no fighting experience and couldn't hide that damn mohawk to keep himself out of danger, a criminal to watch his back—whether he went with them or stayed at home—and a girl from centuries ago who would be watching his progress with her talking cat.

He had a killer headache coming on. And it would only get worse. He was also out of time.

"Here, bro. New prototype field equipment. Your new PP." Milo grinned. "No superspy should leave home without it."

Liev stared at him. "My what?"

Milo grinned. "The new personal port. Don't you like the name?"

"It's not the one we'll market it under."

"That's your problem. I just create this stuff."

"You guys are lucky," Tommy said. "I'd love to be able to invent stuff like this."

Milo looked at Liev, a question in his eyes.

Liev rolled his eyes but gave in … slightly. "We'll see about that, if we all survive this night."

Silence.

Liev glanced at Tommy and was surprised by the hope in his eyes. The kid was like a big puppy, staring at the first bone in his life. And too afraid to hope that it might be for him.

Damn, his life had changed.

CHAPTER 18

LANI SAT IN the kitchen, hugging yet another cup of coffee. Charming was in the bedroom, monitoring Liev's and Milo's progress from there. He was also monitoring Tommy.

Charming—her secret weapon. Tommy had no idea what he'd be up against if he ever attacked her.

She smiled. Then wiped it off her face. She had nothing to smile about. Not until Liev was back again. She should be able to hear his conversation under normal circumstances, but, as Johan's place was still in that weird steel lockdown, they couldn't get audio. She could only watch the figures in the apartment, and that made her insides quiver. Before Liev and Milo left, Milo had quickly explained that the only reason they could see that much was because of what he'd placed inside Johan's apartment last time. She didn't understand it, but it all sounded super cool.

As long as Liev stayed safe. She wished he'd made this a holographic meeting, but apparently Stephen wanted to confirm whoever he was speaking to in person.

It made sense, but it also made the meeting more

dangerous. She took a sip of her coffee and watched Liev's healthy orange splotch on the monitor move around. She understood the other weird looking color was Milo and that he'd done something to mask his presence. He'd wanted to get back into Johan's system for another look. The information he might find had to be incredibly valuable … and dangerous.

These two lived a dangerous life and didn't even appear to notice.

A second orange splotch appeared beside Liev. Shorter, not as orange. "He's arrived," she said excitedly.

Tommy leaned closer for a better look. "I wish we could identify him."

"Maybe we can." She shrugged. "But I'm not sure how." The two splotches seemed to merge, then separate, then merge again.

"Uh, now that looks odd."

"What here doesn't look odd? Are they fighting? Or dancing?" she said, trying to inject humor into the situation, even as her voice wobbled.

"I think …" Tommy stopped, then said in a quizzical voice, "… they are hugging."

"Really?" Her tension eased. Maybe it was Stephen. "Liev said they were good friends."

The two appeared to be standing, facing each other, talking. She watched and waited and waited. Nothing shifted. Then one started to pace. Stephen, the shorter blob. His color darkened and flares fired off his body.

As if he was seriously agitated.

Then he calmed down. And Stephen disappeared.

The light-blue-colored splotch that was Milo joined Liev, then they both disappeared.

The next thing she knew, she was staring up at Liev's bright purple gaze and his open arms.

She ran into them, loving when they closed securely around her. Thank God he was safe.

LIEV HELD LANI close to his heart. All that worry and nothing had happened. Thankfully. He'd told her it would all be fine, but, until it was over, and he was back safe and sound, she wouldn't believe it.

But it was all good now.

"What did he say?"

Liev grimaced. "He thought I was Paul or Tommy here." He motioned at Tommy, standing by the far window. "Stephen already knew that these two were doing special jobs for some of the Council but hadn't figured out who exactly they were working for."

"So Stephen's a good guy?" She waited for his warm smile and nod. "Thank heavens for that." She paused for a moment. "So where does that leave us?"

"Stephen is looking at the Council to help clean house." Liev took a deep breath. "He was fast-tracked into the Council by the elders to find proof of Council wrongdoing."

"A mole!" Charming danced gleefully in place. "So he knows that they are corrupt."

"*Shhh*," she whispered, stealing a glance at Tommy, but he stared out the window, oblivious to the new voice.

"Stephen knows how corrupt they are," Liev said. "He also knows what they did to Tommy, Paul, Gina, Hahn, and Johan. All of it."

Tommy stood up. "And … will he do anything about it?"

"Yes, but not until we get to the bottom of this. He is trying to link Gina's murder to the Council. At least as far as having ordered the hit."

"And by whom?"

Liev winced. "I don't know if I believe him or not, but he seems to think that Hahn did it."

Milo's shocked gasp was loud.

Lani turned to him. "Do you agree or disagree?"

"It's possible." He scowled. "But I'm not sure. I found a lot of information on Johan's computer that I hadn't really looked at because I didn't realize what it was. It's the background information on the Council members and some of their blackmailees. Johan was trying to research them."

"Did he find anything?"

"Hahn had family in the Naturals group. But he had distanced himself from them years ago—about the same time he was accepted into law school."

"And Stephen?" She glanced from one brother to

the other.

Liev nodded. "Stephen was also from the Naturals, but he's years younger than Hahn, so never crossed paths with him. Stephen was one of the few who left for schooling. He was a teen at the time. When he found out that his friends and family had all been killed, he tried to keep his past a secret. He had no idea that he had supposedly died in that particular genocide, and, when he saw his name listed, he just pretended the name was a coincidence and did his best to hide any connection to the group. About a year ago, some Council documents were sent to him, he thinks by Johan, proving that the Council had killed his family."

"Why didn't he say something to you and Milo? Surely he could have asked for your help."

"He wasn't sure what we were into. Milo got into trouble a year ago, for trying to build his first time machine, and he blew out all the power in the city. It was a terrible blackout that caused untold damage to various services and financial institutions. It was an accident, and the Council never could prove it was him, but they always suspected him nonetheless. It meant that Stephen didn't dare approach us because we were already under the Council's watchful eye. It would have looked suspicious, and his actions would have been questioned."

"So now what?"

As he opened his mouth to reply, a boom blasted through the room. The force of the noise picked Lani up and threw her against the counter, like she was a dishrag. Liev was thrown in the same direction, landing half on top of her. As she gasped for air, he rolled over and jumped to his feet—and stared into the unblinking lens of a ComBot standing six inches from him.

His breath sucked in, and he saw the ComBot wasn't alone. A full-on tactical team had been sent to his place.

He tensed. That type of action was saved for the worst of the worst.

As he turned to help Lani, the ComBot said, "Do not move."

Liev froze. His heart still slamming against his ribs, he stared back at the ComBot. "What is your protocol?"

"You are under arrest. For treason."

CHAPTER 19

ONCE AT THE Council building, Liev, Milo, and Lani, along with Tommy off to one side, were shoved into the main chamber. Liev stood stiff and tall in front with Lani, her knees knocking, slightly behind him. She had no idea what the charges stemmed from but thought it had something to do with Tommy's presence in Liev's place. Harboring a criminal or some such thing.

She glanced over where Tommy sat, his arms pinned behind him and a look of defeat on his face. For Tommy, this was bad. Last strike and all that. Her heart still pounded away in her chest, and her palms continued to sweat. Who was she kidding? She was terrified herself. And she was worried about Charming. She hadn't had a chance to say anything to him before they were ported out of the apartment.

Did he even know what had happened?

She'd never trust the authorities in this time period if they could appear in someone's home, swoop them up, and bring them here without just cause.

Liev had tried to explain that it had something to do with terrorist charges, but no way in hell they were terrorists.

He'd told her to not worry, but she couldn't see how to avoid it. His lawyers were dead, and, if others were left to man the firm, they were likely corrupt. His best friend was dead, and he'd been blackmailed into doing criminal activities at the Council's whim, where Liev's other friend was part of this same Council that had had them *retrieved*.

Suspicious, indeed.

Yet strangely, Milo had been allowed to keep his personal comp. He'd been working away on it ever since. Liev had also been able to send several messages. If she only knew who he'd contacted, she might feel better.

She hoped it was that powerful family he'd alluded to. Liev could sure use some help right now.

A commotion at the door heralded the arrival of a dozen suited men. All in black. She almost smiled with relief to see men dressed in power suits and not skin suits.

She stepped forward and slipped her hand into Liev's. He smiled down at her. "It'll be fine."

"You said that already," she muttered.

He squeezed her hand. "And I meant it."

"What kind of place allows that kind of invasive maneuvers without just cause?" she whispered. Several ComBots stood beside her.

One turned to explain. "You are charged with terrorism. You no longer have rights."

"Then, since you entered our home without warning, without a search warrant or any other legal process in place, you are now charged with terrorism," she snapped.

The ComBot looked at her. Then looked at Liev, who was trying to hide his smile, and then back at her. "That is not possible."

"If what you did to me is possible, then what I am doing to you is possible," she cried out. "Or have you not heard of a citizen's arrest?"

The ComBot stared, then lifted his hand unit and asked for direction.

A computerized voice answered, "You are not under arrest. Man your post."

The eldest of the Council members—Liev said his name was Carlson—stood up. "Lani Summerland Blackburn. Step forward."

Lani whispered to Liev, "Do I have to?"

"Yes." He gave her a gentle nudge.

Fine. Then she'd do it her way. "Lani Summerland Blackburn, following orders like a ComBot." And she took two steps to stand front and center. A choked twitter rustled through the room.

"You mock us?" Carlson put on glasses and studied her. After a moment, he frowned and took them off again.

She glared at him. "Can't run your secret scans on me, huh?"

Silence. His face reddened. "You will show respect

here, young lady, or face the consequences."

Lani didn't know where her anger came from; something more like rage bubbled up from deep inside. "Respect? For you? For a corrupt Council? For men who have ordered repeated genocides of a complete group of people for no other reason than they chose to live life differently?" Her voice rang out. "This group of men, this Council, you included, ordered those executions, the annihilation of all the Naturals."

The Councilman slapped a hand over his heart. The other Council members gasped, fear and anger building across the group so strongly that she felt their waves of emotions. Carlson straightened, fury building on his face, but Lani stood tall, not backing down.

After all, she'd been ripped out of her twenty-first-century home, watched as her cat received the knowledge enhancements she had desperately wanted for herself, and still she'd made the best of it by finding her love of a lifetime in Liev two centuries down the road. She had made *that* work. ... Now this? This *corrupt* Council threatened to take it all away from her?

She had nothing to lose.

"You will not hide your murderous soul from me or from the rest of the world. You will not hide your ordering of the slaughter of men, women, and children—the fringe group you call the Naturals—at the flick of your stuck-up, white-ass finger."

Shock hit the Council members.

She rolled right over them as they opened their

mouths, and words ripped out of her from deep inside the pit of her gut, her voice filling the massive chamber. "The world will know of your black hearts and even blacker actions. You had Gina Stewart murdered. Because of you, Johan Strand is dead. And Hahn Driscoll is too, as is Paul Defino. You abused your power and position to corrupt this place—a place of goodness, of fairness—and this place full of people who want nothing more than to live fulfilling lives free of your corrupt rule. How dare you, sir."

Lani had run out of steam, but her ire kept the stick in her backbone in place as an overwhelming silence filled the great hall.

She lifted her chin. She'd be damned if she'd back down now.

Stephen stepped up onto the Council dais. His calm, very serious voice carried in the silence. "Lani Summerland Blackburn, these are very serious charges. Do you have proof to back up your accusations?"

She smiled directly at Carlson, an icy movement that had the man twitching on the spot, the others cringing for what she'd say next. For all her anger, this was a pivotal moment in history, and she, Lani Summerland—no—Lani Blackburn, would make sure it was done right. It seemed this world was desperately in need of a champion. And it had found one—in her. "I was hoping you'd ask that."

She spun and stared at Milo.

He'd changed her life so much, and she'd gradually

forgiven him for everything he'd done these past few days—but, if he couldn't produce the material she needed at her fingertips right at this moment, she would kill him herself.

The ComBots wouldn't get a chance.

He'd be dead before they ever reached him.

"Milo?"

He nodded and clicked away on a few buttons. Instantly a huge—as in, back up several steps before she became part of the monitor display and ended up looking like a female version of Charming's electrified cotton ball—*huge* monitor display materialized.

A video of the slaughter, memos of the orders, names of the dead, emails and texts, all implicating the four top-tier men on the Council in front of her, rolled in an endless display for all to see. A growing murmur of horror swept through the audience.

"Send this out to the world, Milo," she ordered. "Take over every goddamned computer and vid screen in offices and in homes, on computerized ads, and any other place where it can be viewed across the world. Bounce it across every satellite in orbit. Let the people see how power corrupts. Let them see how these four men have shamed their positions, how they have lied and cheated and killed in the name of their own heartless selves."

"In progress," Milo said. "It's streaming out to the world now."

"Stop him," Carlson screamed. "ComBots, stop

this. Remove these criminals from the chamber." The Councilman stood tall, waving his arms around. "Return this chamber to order. I command you."

The ComBots stared back but did not move.

Lani grinned. Probably Milo's doing. She turned to look at the ComBots, standing like a solid army at her side. "Good. You should never follow orders that are just plain bad."

She looked around to find everyone staring at the huge display of data. Horrible mind-numbing numbers, showing a data compilation of a humanity-gone-wrong. She spun back to face the Council and found a team of ComBots standing behind the four men on the Council.

Stephen stood off to one side. She caught his eye. He gave her a smile and saluted her.

Her gaze widened, and she became flustered.

A sound started in the chamber. First low and quiet, then it quickly built in volume. She didn't understand the noise at first over the buzz from the massive monitor at her side.

Then she recognized it.

Clapping.

She turned in a slow movement to find the Council chambers filled to overflowing with men and women of all ages. And they were all clapping. More than that, they were all staring at her.

Her astonished gaze went from face to face. Maybe she was slow but really? Were these people clapping for her?

Her gaze landed on Liev, pride swelling his chest, a wide grin on his face, as he clapped harder than anyone.

Milo. Tommy. Stephen. They were clapping for her.

Tears crept into her eyes.

Maybe she could do something special in this lifetime after all.

She smiled through her tears and waved.

The crowd erupted into cheers.

LIEV COULDN'T BELIEVE that calm, quiet Lani had stood up to the Council, talking, … no, … berating, as in damn-near shouting as she hurled accusations, heaping shame on the Council that had never faced verbal opposition like this before.

The Council had had so much power for so long that they were accustomed to complete obedience, and that had been the chink in their armor. They didn't know what to do with her.

Or how to stop her.

When she hooked Milo into showing everyone the damaging evidence, even the ComBots had shut down. Although Liev cast a suspicious eye at Milo. He might have been behind that too.

This Council was finished.

The individual members would pay heavily for their

crimes against humanity. Lani was right. These men had defiled their way of life. Committing the ultimate sin in the name of power.

Stephen was a shoo-in as a member for the new Council. That was a good thing. He was a fair man.

Liev had been incredibly angered at being hauled down to the Council like a common criminal. Sure, he'd crossed the line—or at least dipped his toe over the line. He'd had to protect his own. That wasn't justification. It was an explanation. He knew why, and the reason still stood. If need be, he'd do it again.

But to see Lani stand so defiantly before their most honored—and corrupt—government system and to systematically rip them to shreds, publicly exposing their grievous deeds to the world? … Well, he wanted to thank the ComBots for bringing him, … them, … here.

To have a front-row view to watch the fall of the Council.

This was a great day.

And to think Lani had brought about the necessary change they'd so badly needed.

Innocent Lani, who'd been dubbed a Natural for no reason of her making, … had picked up the cause and sought justice for her fellow man.

He'd never been prouder.

And she'd never live down this moment.

She'd become an icon now.

Milo, he knew, had already sent the video of her

speech worldwide. Maybe a dangerous thing to do, but, after this, she wouldn't need to hide anymore—except from her adoring fans.

She wouldn't need to cringe when someone spoke to her. Everyone would assume she didn't know much about their world because she had been part of one of the fringe groups. And being one would no longer be a negative trait. She'd elevated the fringe groups to equals. Something they'd never likely understand as they didn't care.

But it was a good thing—especially for her.

Lani had been amazing.

When the clapping started, Liev had been one of the first to join in. When she'd lifted a hand in the air to wave, he'd cheered with the crowd. He'd loved her before this, but now his heart swelled and was ready to burst.

To think he'd worried that she would not find her place in his world. Instead, she'd shown the rest of the world what really mattered.

Respect. Honor. Justice.

Truly, he loved her, this beloved woman of his.

He stepped forward, cheers ringing through his ears, and tugged Lani into his arms.

Dimly, in the background, the cheers resounded louder and louder in approval. He picked her up and twirled her around and cried out to the world, "Damn, I'm a lucky man."

She wrapped her arms tight around his neck, her

breath warm and sexy against his ear as she whispered, "And I'll keep reminding you of it every day of our lives."

He roared with laughter and squeezed her tight. Just then his wrist unit beeped. He glanced over to see Charming's face filling the screen. Liev smirked again. "Lani, look who wants in on the action."

He watched as she caught sight of Charming's face, a huge smile breaking across her beautiful features. "Charming," she cried out.

"About time you contacted me," Charming said, pouting. "You left me all alone."

"I'm sorry. I didn't get a chance to tell you." She rushed to tell him. "The ComBots took us away within seconds."

He sniffed the air, his flat nose going sky-high. "And you couldn't tell me when you had a chance? Jeez, I had to find out from Milo."

"We're coming home," she said. "Soon."

"Sure you are." He scowled. "Like you promised to never leave me alone again?"

"I didn't want to. Honest."

She gave Charming a breathtaking smile so full of love that Liev felt a twinge of jealousy. But he rejected it. There was room in her heart for both of them.

"I'll make it up to you," she said. "I promise."

The cat eyed her carefully, and Liev frowned. Was something devious moving in the back of Charming's big marble eyes?

"Okay, I'll forgive you, if ..."

She frowned suspiciously. "If what?"

He beamed a huge crafty smile at her. "If you bring me home something special. Tuna or shrimp would be good. Lobster?" He flopped to one side in front to the monitor. "You've been gone so long that I was afraid you weren't coming back. I'm starving ..." He moaned. "*Feeeed meeeee.*"

This concludes Book 3 of Broken Protocols:
Cat's Cradle.

Read the first chapter of Book 4 of Broken Protocols:
Cat's Claus below.

Broken Protocols: Cat's Claus (Book #4)
Chapter 1

"WHEN IS CHRISTMAS?" Charming asked.

Lani Blackburn looked at her beloved orange Persian cat and grinned. It was a little hard to have any respect for his vast intelligence when he was upside down, four paws to the wind, and twisted in a bizarre curl.

"Remember? They don't do any of those old holidays anymore."

"So? That's them. Then there's us." He snorted out a sneeze and flopped over on one side. "And the two don't have to be the same."

Sometimes the darnedest things came out of that cat's mouth. And where was this all coming from? "Are you missing the holidays?" She quirked her lips and laughed. "You hated the noise, the company. Really howled when I sang Christmas carols."

"Ha!" He rolled over to glare at her. "Anyone would howl at your singing."

While she was still gasping at his barb, he continued, "I liked the tree. It was fun. Adored the tinsel." He grinned evilly. "Loved the cookies."

She remembered the last Christmas in Technicolor memories. Charming climbing up the pathetic fake tree, until it collapsed on top of him. The problem of him constantly trying to eat the tinsel and her finding the tinsel and plastic needles everywhere, but the cookies? … She groaned out loud. "You used to take a bite out of every one."

"I had to see which one I wanted," he said in such a reasonable tone of voice that she had to laugh.

"Christmas tree? Tinsel?" Liev, Lani's husband, who was technically a couple hundred years younger than her, sat down on her chair with her. She grinned, as the furniture stretched and sprawled to accommodate the extra person. That never got old. Her *husband*—and what a trip that still was to say or to contemplate—held a mug of something hot.

"Is that coffee?" she asked accusingly. "And you didn't bring me one?"

He leaned over and kissed her. "I brought enough to share."

"*Blech.*" Charming rolled over in such a way that his butt was presented.

"Charming, don't you fire that thing," Liev warned.

But gentle snores were already working up and out of her beloved dust ball of a cat.

"Christmas," she murmured, images of past holidays floating through her head. She didn't even know what time of year it was right now. They were currently on a Pacific island paradise. After all the hell they'd been through getting here, she'd wanted nothing more than to crash in peace and to recuperate after her time-traveling side effects—something that was taking longer than expected.

Her body still hadn't fully adjusted to her new surroundings or the atmosphere a couple centuries in the future. Neither had Charming's. And their original trip here to this time era hadn't exactly been a fun one—or one she'd agreed to. But Milo, Liev's genius kid brother, had devised a computer program that had snatched her from the twenty-first century and dumped her here two hundred or so years later, practically in Liev's arms as a gift for him. Thank goodness she'd been holding Charming at the time. Milo had added enhancements for her to better adjust to her new life, only he hadn't known to adjust his calculations for Charming. As a result, Charming had been given enhanced communication skills.

Lani wished she'd have gotten something because not only could Charming talk but he was a wizard when it came to the latest technology.

He matched Milo perfectly.

Affectionately Lani glanced at Milo. His massive mohawk was orange now. She couldn't help but wonder if it wasn't to show his solidarity with Charming. She wouldn't put it past him.

Both Liev and Milo had decent relationships with their family, but it was distant. Then again, that might have been because of genius Milo's work. The security around the two men was something else. Milo had a seriously scary brain. When he'd created the time-travel program that had hauled her out of her life, he'd created a hell of a mess.

Now he was working on something else. Genius was to be allowed at all times, as Milo had created some amazing inventions, but genius also needed to be watched. Up until now, Liev kept tabs on his brother, like a hen trying to keep track of twenty chicks. It worked but not well.

"What are you doing, Milo?"

"Research."

"Of course," she said patiently. "Research on what?"

She tugged Liev's mug toward her and took a sip. The one thing they did wonderfully well in this century was coffee. Lord, it was good. Travel was another one. Planes had been relegated to the annals of history, as the dirigibles had been in her time. Now they could punch in a code and walk through a portal. She loved that.

And she'd quickly fallen in love with her new husband. Their relationship was in its early stages for them though. A honeymoon phase, so to speak. Still, as honeymoons went, it was pretty great, once they'd gotten over the attacks, attempted kidnappings, and murders that had arisen after her time-travel event.

She smiled.

"What's that look for?" Liev glanced at her, his eyes warming.

"You. Us." She loved that about him. He hadn't had much long-term relationship experience before she'd landed almost literally in his lap, but he'd blossomed since.

So had she. She felt blessed to have him in her life.

Maybe the other two felt the same as well. The four of them made up their family unit. She knew a few people she might one day learn to call friends, but, because of the many pitfalls in this new life waiting to trip her up, she was hesitant to get cozy with anyone. After all, the conversations were limited to keep her past a secret. Then again, she'd also gained some notoriety recently, and many people had heard of her by now.

How weird was that?

Cool too. She'd been transformed from a number in a city of big numbers to someone special here.

She'd still rather trade it all in for the ability to navigate the minefields that awaited her. She didn't understand the most basic things here.

"Christmas."

Milo's distracted voice pulled her from her musings. "Christmas?" She shook her head. "You don't do any holidays anymore, do you?"

"No. Too many protests from dissident groups all the time. As the protests became more violent, we had to ban more and more of them. Now they don't exist."

Holidays gave people something to look forward to, something to celebrate. Who in a normal workforce didn't love the thought of getting an extra day off because the holidays were coming? And the thought of family and friends gathering for Thanksgiving and Christmas—two of the biggest holidays in her time—made her reminisce about the past.

It was sad in a way. No special neighborhood gatherings or celebrations had happened since she'd arrived here. Families apparently tried to get together on a regular basis, but she could easily see how that would go by the wayside very quickly as everyone's lives ramped up.

The thought of missing Christmas put Lani in a melancholy mood.

She had great memories. Even alone with Charming, they'd had fun. She'd put treats on top of the tree, and he would climb up the needle-covered branches time and time again. Sometimes it worked well and sometimes not so well. she'd laughed a lot, sometimes cried, but they'd had each other. Lani had had Christmas parties at work too. Yeah, those memories brought a wince to her face, but at least they'd been memorable.

"What was Christmas all about?" Liev asked, his tone curious.

"Togetherness," she said instantly. "Family. Friends. Rejoicing in the experience of being alive and sharing what you had with others."

She smiled reassuringly at him. Okay, so it was a little smile, but her lips did twitch, so it counted. Liev worried about her. Always. He was wonderfully considerate. And she loved every minute of it.

A huge diesel engine kicked in. She glanced over to find Charming grinning at her upside down. She reached for him and rubbed his tummy. "You loved the turkey dinners."

"And the gravy."

She didn't think it was possible, but Charming's grin widened. Then his eyes turned huge. "Is it lunchtime? Did I miss lunch?" He rolled over and snapped to his feet. His gaze locked onto poor Liev, and, if Charming could have mentally forced Liev to get up and feed him, he would have.

A side effect of the time travel.

Her appetite was not as ravenous as Charming's, but now that Charming had brought up food, her stomach growled in sympathy. Charming turned to look her way, and his grin widened. He knew Liev might ignore her cat's demands for food, but he'd never ignore Lani's.

"Fine, food it is then."

"Thanks, Liev." She accepted the still half-full mug of coffee from him and sat back. Another great thing about her relationship was that Liev loved to cook. In a world of automatic food, it was his hobby. He cooked the same way people in her time did. Not her, of course. She'd had a penchant for fast food and pizza, whereas Milo had a preference for those disgusting health shakes.

She shuddered just thinking about them. She and Charming had been forced to drink them in the beginning to help them recover. Not fun.

But now, with Liev looking after them as well as he did, she knew they'd both landed on their feet in a clover patch.

Life was good.

LIEV WANDERED INTO the kitchen to sort out a meal for everyone. *Everyone* being the four of them. Milo might join them, but he ate like a bird. Charming, on the other hand, ate like a tiger. So odd.

Still, Liev hummed in the space he'd had renovated to suit his needs, which essentially mimicked his kitchen at home, and pulled out the makings for big thick sandwiches on fresh bread. As he cut the bread, his mind drifted to the Christmas issue. Not only did his century have no religious or fun holiday traditions, like Lani had grown up with, but no celebrations to look forward to either, like she'd also mentioned. He vaguely remembered seeing something about the holidays in his history lessons. That had been a long time ago. He'd most likely downloaded them and assimilated the information into his brain without considering the significance of it. As it had no relevance to his life at the time, he had stuffed it back into his deepest memories. Now, he not only wished he'd paid more attention but he wondered just what he'd missed out on himself.

His childhood hadn't been lonely per se, but it hadn't been overwhelming with love and fun either. He'd taken over Milo's care at an early age after their parents' death. That had taken all the fun out of his life. Milo even seemed to have stopped his mental development at the age of sixteen. And that took a lot of patience. With Lani joining their tiny family unit, Milo had mellowed out and had fallen into line in many ways, accepting the feminine rules without argument. Lani even convinced him to join them for meals, so they could have family time.

Liev hadn't really understood what that meant, but he cherished the time she'd carved out for the four of them. Yes, he included Charming in that group. Good luck keeping him out. They did have to work on his manners though. Lani tried, but, any time she got distracted, Charming would sneak food off her plate and scarf it down before she had a chance to stop him. Even when Liev doubled the cat's portions, Charming would still pull the same tricks.

As a result, Liev had dialed down the portions—much to Charming's disgust. Even now, Liev could feel those huge golden orbs locked on his every movement as he made lunch. He had made an egg salad yesterday, which remained in the fridge. It was an old-fashioned recipe with pickles in it. He'd had to scrounge those from a specialty shop, and it had cost a fortune.

At least he had one of those.

And as long as Milo continued to devise the wild and wonderful things he invented, that wouldn't change anytime soon.

"Lani, Liev is daydreaming again," Charming tattled.

Liev shook his head at Charming's not-so-subtle way of saying Liev was slow to bring the food to the table. Lani might be working on the cat's manners, but a lot of improvement was left to be had. Liev grinned.

He and Milo had both lived a bachelor lifestyle, and, wow, had that changed.

In a good way—at least for Liev. He glanced at his kid brother to see him muttering like crazy over his screen.

Liev frowned when he realized that the screen on this side of the monitor had been blacked out, so no one could see what Milo was doing. Studying his genius brother's features, Liev figured Milo was just deep into his research and turned back to making lunch. Bringing out a fresh pineapple that he'd paid an exorbitant price for, Liev quickly prepped it and portioned it out.

"Lani said she'd trade her egg salad for my pineapple," Charming piped up with a hopeful look.

Liev shook his head. "I wasn't giving you pineapple to begin with."

"Then I'd better be getting more than my fair share of egg salad," he groused.

Liev grinned like an idiot. How had his staid, stressed-out, overworked life become this combination of a loving, laughing lifestyle instead?

Just lucky, he guessed.

"Milo, come join us. We're sitting down to eat," Liev said, as he finished plating the food.

"Be there in a minute."

Liev walked to the table and held the plates up until Lani made it to her seat. Otherwise Charming—precariously balanced on his back legs—would have tried to take the plate with the bigger portions.

When safe, Liev placed the plates down and took his own seat.

Minutes later Milo joined them, one of his nasty all-natural green good-for-you-if-you-can-get-it-down concoctions sitting in front of him.

Liev caught sight of Milo's gaze and followed it back to the opposite side of the table. He stared in horrified fascination as Charming tore into the pile of chopped eggs on his plate. Bits and pieces were spilling off his chin and back onto his plate, much of it falling onto the surrounding table.

Even Lani stared.

Charming finally noticed. He lifted his head, surveyed the mess, rolled his eyes, and tried to clean it up a little. Then, as if realizing he would just make more of a mess soon, he shot them a dirty look and went back to eating the way he'd been before.

"Just one big happy family," Liev murmured.

"And aren't you blessed?" Lani laughed.

"I so am."

Book 4 is available now!

To find out more visit Dale Mayer's website.

https://geni.us/DMClausUniversal

Arsenic in the Azaleas

A new cozy mystery series from USA Today best-selling author Dale Mayer. Follow gardener and amateur sleuth Doreen Montgomery—and her amusing and mostly lovable cat, dog, and parrot—as they catch murderers and solve crimes in lovely Kelowna, British Columbia.

Riches to rags. ... Controlling to chaos. ... But murder ... seriously?

After her ex-husband leaves her high and dry, former socialite Doreen Montgomery's chance at a new life comes in the form of her grandmother, Nan's, dilapidated old house in picturesque Kelowna ... and the added job of caring for the animals Nan couldn't take into assisted living with her: Thaddeus, the loquacious African gray parrot with a ripe vocabulary, and his buddy, Goliath, a monster-size cat with an equally monstrous attitude.

It's the new start Doreen and her beloved basset hound, Mugs, desperately need. But, just as things start to look up for Doreen, Goliath the cat and Mugs the dog find a human finger in Nan's overrun garden.

And not just a finger. Once the police start digging, the rest of the body turns up and turns out to be connected to an old unsolved crime.

With her grandmother as the prime suspect, Doreen soon finds herself stumbling over clues and getting on Corporal Mack Moreau's last nerve, as she does her best to prove her beloved Nan innocent of murder.

Arsenic in the Azaleas is available now!
To find out more visit Dale Mayer's website.
https://geni.us/DMArsenicUniversal

Author's Note

Thank you for reading Cat's Cradle! If you enjoyed my book, I'd appreciate it if you'd leave a review.

Dear reader,

I love to hear from readers, and you can contact me at my website: www.dalemayer.com or at my Facebook author page. To be informed of new releases and special offers, sign up for my newsletter or follow me on BookBub. And if you are interested in joining Dale Mayer's Reader Group, here is the Facebook sign up page.
http://geni.us/DaleMayerFBGroup

Cheers,
Dale Mayer

About the Author

Dale Mayer is a *USA Today* best-selling author, best known for her SEALs military romances, her Psychic Visions series, and her Lovely Lethal Garden cozy series. Her contemporary romances are raw and full of passion and emotion (Broken But … Mending, Hathaway House series). Her thrillers will keep you guessing (Kate Morgan, By Death series), and her romantic comedies will keep you giggling (*It's a Dog's Life*, a stand-alone novella; and the Broken Protocols series, starring Charming Marvin, the cat).

Dale honors the stories that come to her—and some of them are crazy, break all the rules and cross multiple genres!

To go with her fiction, she also writes nonfiction in many different fields, with books available on résumé writing, companion gardening, and the US mortgage system. All her books are available in print and ebook format.

Connect with Dale Mayer Online

Dale's Website – www.dalemayer.com
Twitter – @DaleMayer
Facebook Page – geni.us/DaleMayerFBFanPage
Facebook Group – geni.us/DaleMayerFBGroup
BookBub – geni.us/DaleMayerBookbub
Instagram – geni.us/DaleMayerInstagram
Goodreads – geni.us/DaleMayerGoodreads
Newsletter – geni.us/DaleNews

Also by Dale Mayer

Published Adult Books:

Hathaway House
Aaron, Book 1
Brock, Book 2
Cole, Book 3
Denton, Book 4
Elliot, Book 5
Finn, Book 6
Gregory, Book 7
Heath, Book 8
Iain, Book 9
Jaden, Book 10
Keith, Book 11

The K9 Files
Ethan, Book 1
Pierce, Book 2
Zane, Book 3
Blaze, Book 4
Lucas, Book 5
Parker, Book 6
Carter, Book 7
Weston, Book 8

Lovely Lethal Gardens

Arsenic in the Azaleas, Book 1

Bones in the Begonias, Book 2

Corpse in the Carnations, Book 3

Daggers in the Dahlias, Book 4

Evidence in the Echinacea, Book 5

Footprints in the Ferns, Book 6

Gun in the Gardenias, Book 7

Handcuffs in the Heather, Book 8

Ice Pick in the Ivy, Book 9

Psychic Vision Series

Tuesday's Child

Hide 'n Go Seek

Maddy's Floor

Garden of Sorrow

Knock Knock…

Rare Find

Eyes to the Soul

Now You See Her

Shattered

Into the Abyss

Seeds of Malice

Eye of the Falcon

Itsy-Bitsy Spider

Unmasked

Deep Beneath

From the Ashes

Stroke of Death

Psychic Visions Books 1–3

Psychic Visions Books 4–6
Psychic Visions Books 7–9

By Death Series
Touched by Death
Haunted by Death
Chilled by Death
By Death Books 1–3

Broken Protocols – Romantic Comedy Series
Cat's Meow
Cat's Pajamas
Cat's Cradle
Cat's Claus
Broken Protocols 1-4

Broken and... Mending
Skin
Scars
Scales (of Justice)
Broken but... Mending 1-3

Glory
Genesis
Tori
Celeste
Glory Trilogy

Biker Blues
Morgan: Biker Blues, Volume 1
Cash: Biker Blues, Volume 2

Heroes for Hire, Books 13–15

SEALs of Steel

Badger: SEALs of Steel, Book 1
Erick: SEALs of Steel, Book 2
Cade: SEALs of Steel, Book 3
Talon: SEALs of Steel, Book 4
Laszlo: SEALs of Steel, Book 5
Geir: SEALs of Steel, Book 6
Jager: SEALs of Steel, Book 7
The Final Reveal: SEALs of Steel, Book 8
SEALs of Steel, Books 1–4
SEALs of Steel, Books 5–8
SEALs of Steel, Books 1–8

The Mavericks

Kerrick, Book 1
Griffin, Book 2
Jax, Book 3
Beau, Book 4
Asher, Book 5
Ryker, Book 6
Miles, Book 7
Nico, Book 8
Keane, Book 9
Lennox, Book 10
Gavin, Book 11
Shane, Book 12

Bullard's Battle Series

Ryland's Reach, Book 1

Cain's Cross, Book 2

Eton's Escape, Book 3

Garret's Gambit, Book 4

Kano's Keep, Book 5

Fallon's Flaw, Book 6

Quinn's Quest, Book 7

Bullard's Beauty, Book 8

Collections

Dare to Be You…

Dare to Love…

Dare to be Strong…

RomanceX3

Standalone Novellas

It's a Dog's Life

Riana's Revenge

Second Chances

Published Young Adult Books:

Family Blood Ties Series

Vampire in Denial

Vampire in Distress

Vampire in Design

Vampire in Deceit

Vampire in Defiance

Vampire in Conflict

Vampire in Chaos

Vampire in Crisis

Vampire in Control

Vampire in Charge

Family Blood Ties Set 1–3

Family Blood Ties Set 1–5

Family Blood Ties Set 4–6

Family Blood Ties Set 7–9

Sian's Solution, A Family Blood Ties Series Prequel Novelette

Design series

Dangerous Designs

Deadly Designs

Darkest Designs

Design Series Trilogy

Standalone

In Cassie's Corner

Gem Stone (a Gemma Stone Mystery)

Time Thieves

Published Non-Fiction Books:

Career Essentials

Career Essentials: The Résumé

Career Essentials: The Cover Letter

Career Essentials: The Interview

Career Essentials: 3 in 1

www.ingramcontent.com/pod-product-compliance
Lightning Source LLC
Chambersburg PA
CBHW071412100726
47908CB00004B/1149